TOLETIS

TOLETIS

Rafa Ruiz

Illustrated by Elena Hormiga
Translated by Ben Dawlatly

Neem Tree
PRESS

Neem Tree Press Limited, 1st Floor
2 Woodberry Grove, London, N12 0DR, UK

Published by Neem Tree Press Limited 2017
www.neemtreepress.com
info@neemtreepress.com

Text copyright © Rafa Ruiz, 2010
Illustrations copyright © Elena Hormiga, 2014
Translation copyright © Ben Dawlatly, 2017
This edition © Neem Tree Press Limited, 2017
First Imprint 2017

A catalogue record for this book is available from the British Library
ISBN 978-1-911107-14-9

Printed and bound in Great Britain
by Short Run Press Limited, Exeter, Devon

MIX
Paper from
responsible sources
FSC
www.fsc.org
FSC® C014540

TABLE OF CONTENTS

1

Spring

RA'S APPLE TREES

When he was four or five years old, someone in his family lovingly called him a toll collector, referring to his habit of asking for various household items which he needed for his adventures, and not letting anybody get on with their day until he had the objects. He quite liked the nickname, but he wanted to adapt it a little, inspired by what he'd learnt in a book on Ancient Egypt. What so amazed him about the sphinxes and hieroglyphs, the jackal-, hawk- and ibis-headed gods was that animals and nature seemed to pervade everything in that culture. He took the 'toll', dropped the 'collector', and settled on Toletis. It sounded both familiar and pharaonic. Yes, he liked the name Toletis a lot.

When speaking to his Grandfather Rafael, who was always everywhere, he called him Ra, like the sun god of the Egyptians. And Toletis's Spanish water dog, whose shiny eyes you could hardly see, was christened Amenophis. Although, since he'd heard that dogs only understand vowels and tones, and not consonants, and seeing as Amenophis was such a long name, most of the time he just called him Aeoi, or even Ae. Other times he would test the theory by saying Capeloti, Tatetoti or Mamemoni … and it worked. Amenophis would come running over as long as the right vowels were said in the right order. His best friend, Andy, got the name Tutankhamun, simply because Toletis would so often say, 'I'm going out to play. You too? You too? You Tutankhamun.'

Andy was not in the habit of going against the grain; he had so many brothers – seven – with such different opinions, that in order to not spend the day arguing, he'd become accustomed to spending his time observing a lot, keeping quiet, and, little by little, silently getting away with things. That, and the way he blinked so slowly, gave him a permanent expression of tiredness. So, he agreed to the name. To keep it simple, Toletis often shortened it to Tutan.

They wanted to bring Claudia into the Pharaoh group, the girl with the huge tangled mane who had arrived in town with her parents to set up an eco-tourism hostel, and who was great fun to hang out with. But Toletis couldn't find an elegant solution. He was unable to think of any names beginning with 'She', 'Her' or 'Girl' that were intriguing – and she deserved an intriguing name – and which also sounded Egyptian. The best they could come up with was Shefertiti, which was reminiscent of Queen Nefertiti, the one with the long neck pictured in all the books on Egypt, but in the end they decided to leave it as it was, as Claudia. At the end of the day, it was a pretty cool name, and they all thought it sounded like it was from another ancient empire: Rome.

He had learnt many things from his Grandfather, Ra. But one thing above all: to consider nature as a thinking, sentient being who breathes and laughs, cries and talks, and who teaches us many lessons, whether or not we want to learn them or are clever enough to understand them. Toletis would never forget the first thing his Grandfather used to ask him every morning, as soon as he woke up: 'What's the day doing today?' Because his Grandfather always told him that whether it rains or snows or the sun shines hot, it's not chance but intent; something that nature wants to do, because she has decided it should be like that. She's naturally talented at putting the mystery into the mountains, adorning the towns, turning the wheat golden, or heating up the rabbits' warrens.

For as long as Toletis could remember, he'd been less interested in the gossip and hubbub of his small, sprawling town than in the hills and forests that surrounded it. The town itself had suffered quite a bit in the time he had known it. The trees had been stripped, little by little: first a fire, then a road, then the widening of the road, and then some logging to sell the lumber and raise money to fix the town hall, and then the plague that killed all the elms. In short, the verdant town nestled in the mountains where Toletis had been born had become somewhat gloomy and dreary, with hardly any nooks and crannies for playing hide-and-seek. That's why the apple tree plan came about.

Toletis would obviously have liked to have many kinds of trees in his town: birches, ashes, oaks, beeches, chestnuts, maples, willows, and lime trees. But planting apple trees was quite a bit simpler, because their fruits, and therefore their seeds, were in the children's lunchboxes every day. What's more, Toletis would get mixed up when it came to the other trees. He could tell an apple tree straight away, but was never sure about the rest.

Once, he tried to learn them all by heart – when he was five years old, more or less when people started calling him Toletis, and when there were still trees in his town – and he almost turned green. Ra taught

him the names of the different trees, and so that he didn't forget them, he decided to try and remember the information by tasting the leaves. That week he ate a ton of leaves: black poplar, oak, beech, chestnut, and elm. Until he noticed that his tongue was turning green. Tutankhamun let him know that green marks were also appearing behind his ears. Toletis never knew whether Tutan was telling the truth or joking. But just in case, and before he ended up looking like a lettuce, he decided to stop eating leaves.

That incident and the steady disappearance of the trees meant that he never managed to learn their names. And Toletis couldn't get an idea of what each tree was really like from the photos in the encyclopaedias at home. There was nothing in the books about the sounds the different leaves made when the wind blew through them, the places where the trees themselves preferred to grow, and the birds that most liked to make their homes in them; all crucial points for really knowing the different trees, Toletis thought. His parents would exchange concerned glances when they saw their son frantically leafing through textbooks with a puzzled look on his face. Or he would mutter ferociously about the fact that he could never find any documentaries on TV about trees: they were almost always about bears, lions and elephants!

Toletis never imagined it could be so hard to plant apple trees. The plan was perfect. Over the course of a week, Claudia, Tutankhamun and he saved the pips from the apples their parents gave them for dessert or for break time at school or just as a snack. And one day, at sunset, in the second week of April, when the town was quiet and they couldn't see any people who would waste their time by asking stupid questions, they grabbed a hoe and some old gardening forks, ready to dig some small holes and chuck the pips in. They thought that with the spring rain, the pips would quickly transform into little apple trees. The plan was perfect, and the time had come to put it in motion.

But suddenly little problems started to appear.

Buxom Aunty Josefina, who wasn't sporting her normal cheeky smile, saw Toletis with a trowel in one hand and a jar of apple seeds in the other, and guessing what he was up to, told him that apple seeds weren't to be sown in the vegetable patch:

'Don't you go and blubber it up! Because when the trees grow biggly-wiggly, there'll be too much umbrage, and the broccoli won't sprout, the broad beans won't ripen, and we won't get any big, black boysenberries.' Aunty Josefina really liked using the letter B.

When Prickle-Chin Clement saw Toletis digging a hole in the meadow, he told him not to plant apple trees there either:

'The cows and the mares won't treat them with respect. They'll eat the seedlings, and I don't have the time or the patience to be looking after so many trees.'

Prickly Prickle-Chin Clement belonged to that breed of person that sees life as one immense problem, where each day is an obstacle and everyone else is just there to rub him the wrong way.

Neither in meadows nor in orchards. Toletis and his friends, their gardening tools tucked under their arms, were running out of space in the town. But the warnings and prohibitions still didn't stop.

Ron and his wife, Nora, told Toletis not to plant any trees close to the hedges or the dry stone walls, nor in any alleys or close to any fences, not in amongst the shrubs nor in any corners:

'Brambles, nettles and weeds grow like the cream on boiling milk, and they won't let the saplings get a peep of light. They'll suffocate them and won't let them have any soil for their roots, nor air nor sun for their first shoots.'

Neither here, nor there. Not Ron, nor Nora.

In case any little space had been left out, Aunt Matilda snuffed out Toletis's few remaining hopes. She told him that he couldn't plant apple trees on public land:

'You have to run it past the other neighbours, and you already know that not everybody wants them. Not on other people's farms, because you have to get their permission first. And you definitely can't plant them on our farms … '

'Why not on ours?' asked a shocked Toletis.

'Because apple trees are ugly. Besides, this town is so cold and high up that the apples end up bitter and barely edible.'

'That's not true! Apple trees aren't ugly, and the apples that grow are really delicious.'

'Okay, okay, that's enough fussing. Who'd have thought some blasted trees would be such a nuisance?'

Toletis knew that he could rely only on his Grandfather Ra. When the greatest hindrances appeared, Ra was always ready to help him. An idea lit up inside Toletis's head …

Toletis, Claudia and Tutan counted their collected apple pips. They had 147. They popped them back into the jar and went to see Ra once the sun started to set. Toletis knew that Ra listened to him every day, as the last rays of the setting sun dwindled. His mother had told him so on that especially sad day: 'Grandpa's lights are fading, he's going far away. But don't worry, he'll still be here; from now on he'll watch us from the hilltop with the last shafts of sunlight before nightfall. So, whenever you want to talk to him, just wait until sunset, and if it looks beautiful, that's because he's listening.' Toletis always knew that he could find Ra in amongst the greenery.

Toletis had found himself a quiet corner of a meadow to consult Ra about his problems.

That spring afternoon, everything was tranquil and serene. A bird was singing. The eventide sunbeams shone with their purple-orange hue.

Toletis recounted their plan to his Grandfather, and he waited a while. Tutan and Claudia were studying Toletis more than the sky, and they couldn't fathom how they were going to find a solution to the apple tree plan. Toletis watched the horizon, and Tutan and Claudia watched him.

Suddenly, Toletis shouted, 'Right! That's it! Over there! Where that last ray of sunshine is hitting the ground.'

He instantly knew that he'd been granted permission to plant all the pips in that little patch of land on the hill, all 147 of them.

'Thanks, Ra. You'll see the stupid look on everyone's faces. They don't know anything about what they grow in their gardens.' And he added, 'I hope it rains soon so the apple trees grow healthy and quickly, and Ra can shine down on all his apples.'

'Yeah, I hope it does rain soon, because I'm not going all the way over there to water them. It's a mega uphill hike, and everyone will see us and think we're a bunch of nutcases, and … ' complained Claudia.

'If it doesn't rain, we'll come and water them at night, and bring a couple of bottles each.'

'You can count me out,' Claudia insisted.

But Toletis carried on explaining his plan, ignoring Claudia's qualms, because he was sure, when it came down to it, that she'd be the first to step up for watering duty.

It rained all week, lightly but constantly, so Toletis, Claudia and Tutan didn't have to go and water the apple trees.

On the seventh day, they decided to go and see how the planted apple pips were coming along. They hiked the long uphill slog, and when they finally got to their apple tree nursery, Claudia was almost petrified by what confronted her. It was as if there were little mice everywhere: hundreds of miniature trees were scurrying around at great speed, and

they covered the patch of hillside where the pips had been buried. They hardly made any noise, just a sharp hissing sound. These were definitely not the apple trees they had been expecting to see!

The treenie-weenies, as Claudia called them – she was sometimes prone to being a little sentimental – were frightened of the sight of the children. They huddled together and stayed very still. Each one was like a little bouquet of three or four leaves, held together by a trunk with bark and some dishevelled roots that moved like little legs. The way the leaves moved, it was like they were the arms and head. They were, without a doubt, very strange but friendly and inoffensive beings. Tutankhamun, despite being very clever, tended to ask foolish questions at the most inopportune moments, and as soon as he saw the treenie-weenies, he asked:

'Do you think they bite?'

Toletis eliminated his doubt with another question:

'With what?'

The leaves on each of the plants were different. Toletis was convinced that there were elm, black poplar, willow, oak, beech, pine, ash, lime, fir, maple, birch, and chestnut trees, although he didn't know how to distinguish one from the other.

After the initial moment of surprise in which everybody – treenie-weenies and children – remained frozen and silent, Toletis took the initiative. He took a step forward. The treenie-weenies took three of their tiny steps back.

Tutan had an idea. He always liked imitating the sounds of animals and would spend entire afternoons perfecting his impressions until he managed to get the animals to respond to him. Then he would revel in his success and add the new sound to his repertoire. He had already learnt 17 languages that allowed him to communicate with coots and cows, hens, pigs, sheep, horses, cats, dogs, goldfinches, hen harriers, hares and herons, swallows, swifts, tawny owls, grass hoppers, and his Grandmother's wolfhound. The one that was proving hardest was the language of the magpies. He'd spent three months trying to strike up a conversation with them. With the starlings, however, the complete opposite had occurred. It was the birds that were learning human language without any difficulties.

Tutankhamun was able to say 'good morning' and 'see you tomorrow' to those 17 different animals. He could ask them how they were feeling, if they were hungry and whether they thought it was going to rain, and he could understand if they answered yes or no, or 'leave us alone; we're in a hurry,' a very common response from woodland creatures who are always ridiculously busy and scurrying this way and that.

Without a second thought, Tutankhamun drew on his experience and tried to communicate with the treenie-weenies. He started to hiss. Initially, his tactics were unfruitful. In fact, the treenie-weenies took fright and scrunched into cowering little gem lettuces.

Tutan continued trying, with a sssississsoo here and a ssssoooossssssissi there. Until, after twenty minutes, when he hissed in a very complex way, with more zeds than esses, the treenie-weenies unfurled their arm-leaves and started to murmur amongst themselves.

'That took ages! Now let's see how you manage to make that weird noise again with all those esses and zeds,' Claudia said to him.

For the next two weeks, the kids went to the hill every evening to visit the treenie-weenies and to see if Tutan could learn their delicate language.

By the time May came around and the sun started making the treenie-weenies more unruly and restless, Tutankhamun, luckily, had just about managed to get a handle on their strange dialect. According to what he translated to Claudia and Toletis, the treenie-weenies were the souls of all the trees that had been felled in the town over recent years. All the treenie-weenies needed to find another tree to inhabit, to perpetuate the spirits of the felled trees for the years, decades and centuries to come.

But the treenie-weenies were bored, because the townsfolk were no longer planting new trees, and they didn't even let the existing ones flourish that were growing in the countryside on their own.

Tutankhamun consulted Toletis and Claudia to see if they could find a silver lining and come up with a way to help so many bored tree-souls. Toletis, who was as quick as a gecko whenever it was sunny, instantly knew what to do. Now, in addition to the treenie-weenies running around, healthy and tenacious apple trees were also sprouting from the pips the children had planted in the patch of land that Ra had guided them to. Balmy May days were in full swing with the occasional drizzly afternoon. Toletis's plan was for the apple trees to give the treenie-weenies piggybacks. Even though they'd never done it before, surely each apple tree wouldn't mind if a few treenie-weenies hopped on, as long as they took care not to break the flimsy young branches?

Toletis delivered the instructions:

'Climb on carefully and get yourselves well organised. If any of you are about to fall, the rest should lend a hand so no one gets hurt. And if you find yourself very cramped, stretch your leaves up to the sky to make some space.'

And Tutan, who was speaking the treenie-weenie language much better than he could speak the language of the herons or hares, translated and translated, with an incessant hissing.

He did, however, sometimes get stuck because he didn't know how to transmit some of Toletis's concepts to them: getting hurt and being cramped, for example. But, in the end, through mime he always managed to explain things. It was pleasant to see the treenie-weenies nodding their sort of micro-melon heads up and down in approval.

Claudia often relied on her instincts and sensations; she showed a special tenderness toward anything small, and she insisted on taking the treenie-weenies a bottle of sparkling water, claiming that the fizz would help them grow bubblier. Toletis's argument that the treenie-weenies would probably prefer rainwater, which isn't effervescent, fell on deaf ears.

The next day, it began to rain in the valley like never before, while the sun continued to blaze, too. As a result, the water came down warm and threw out all seven colours of the rainbow, which went down phenomenally with Ra's apple trees. It made them stronger, which was just as well because they had to hold up the chatterbox treenie-weenies who hadn't stopped babbling about the luck they'd had.

And that whole week of May went on like that, the rain falling in colours.

When it stopped raining, one night when the moon was full, the stars were big, and Amenophis was howling, something happened that neither Aunty Josefina, nor Uncle Joseph, nor Prickle-Chin Clement, nor Ron nor Nora, nor Aunty Matilda could understand or explain. They had never seen anything like it nor had they ever heard of anything similar; they didn't even know what to call it. It was as if their imaginations had broken through and fused with the real world.

A giant tree, as tall as 17 or 27 church steeples, had grown from one point on the hillside. The naked eye couldn't see the top of it. It was a gigantic tree made up of many different types of trees, standing one on top of the other. Surrounding them, as to protect them, 146 other apple trees had popped up.

'Oh my gosh! What loons!' let fly Claudia. 'All the treenie-weenies have jumped on the same apple tree. Oh, of course! I get it! They were huddling together to stay warm and not get too wet. And it was hammering it down! Oh my! Oh my! Everybody piggybacking on the same apple tree! How funny, all the treenie-weenies together!'

The one at the bottom of the tower, the only one that was in contact with the earth, was an apple tree. Toletis named him Ra, Ra the apple tree. On top of him were beautiful elms, oaks, chestnuts, willows, and ashes. The trunk of one tree was growing from the canopy of another, and its branches were, in turn, tangled with the roots of the next tree up, which in turn served as the ground for another tree that provided sustenance to another and another and another and another.

The birds liked it, and they flew in the next morning to take their new house on a test run. Seven pairs of herons started building nests there. The mist also fancied mingling with such a marvellous creature, and every evening she would wrap herself gently around the splendid green tower.

Toletis, with the sudden urge of a jubilant gecko, gave three kisses to Claudia, Tutan and Amenophis.

Since that day, Toletis's town has been the one with the most trees in the entire valley, even if they are all gathered in a tower, one on top of the other, touching the earth and tickling the clouds.

2

Spring

A PIECE OF MIST

Toletis made all the important decisions in his life while gazing at Ra's rays or watching the mist tumble head first down the hillsides, covering everything little by little, hushing the town until dusk, bringing refreshing air to summer days and spreading the moisture that brought the geraniums and rose bushes back to life.

Sitting on the grass, in the corner of his favourite meadow, Toletis had become a great admirer of the mist, and he would confess secrets to her that only she could hear and keep. He had confessed, only to the mist and no one else, about the cherries missing from his Grandfather's orchard that had been eaten by just him, all of them.

In return for his loyalty and trust in her, the mist would always envelop him sweetly, wet his brow to keep him calm, and tousle his hair into damp kiss curls. Day by day, Toletis and the mist's friendship grew stronger and stronger.

The mist was so gentle and wise that Toletis decided to capture a piece of that frayed and flossy, white, tender blanket, a piece that would be able to put right some of the town's imperfections. Toletis thought that a piece of magical fluffiness that could quench thirst and wipe away sweat and tiredness could be used for lots of great and important things.

'I need a sheet, Mum,' said Toletis.

'Please go and get one from the attic,' his mother replied.

'No, it can't have any holes in it.'

'Toletis, if it's to play with, an old sheet will do. I'm not going to give you a brand new one just so you can bring it back all torn and dirty.'

'It's not to play with, Mum! It's to gather a piece of mist.'

'Is this another one of your plans, Toletis? And what are you going to do with the mist?'

'Cover nasty things.'

'But it'll evaporate as soon as you catch it, my sweet, way before you get the chance to use it for one of your crazy ideas.'

'No, it won't; I know how to look after it, Mum.'

'Well, fine then, but please don't put it in the fridge. It'll make the fruit smell weird.'

'Relax, Mum, it'll only take two days, anyway.'

'And won't the rest of the mist get angry that you've broken it up and taken a piece away?'

'But it's only going to be a tiny little bit ... Whatever I can fit in a sheet.'

'OK. Go on then, get one from the wardrobe. One of the white ones should do, not the lacy ones. But you have to bring it back in three days, and I don't want a single hole in it.'

'Love you, Mum.'

'Mum is beautiful and kind-hearted,' whispered Toletis, so that he could be heard by all the minuscule beings that inhabit the world around us but whom we rarely see and don't realise we live amongst. He heard a faint squeak of acknowledgment from one of the otherworldly creatures, but it might have just been a mouse on the lookout for a breadcrumb or a dropped peanut.

Claudia went to the riverbank with Toletis to catch the mist. She brought along a big clay casserole pot with a lid, because she also wanted a piece for herself.

Claudia, as well as being dazzling, was a perfectionist and a very practical one at that.

Toletis hung the sheet up vertically between two hawthorn bushes. Claudia took the lid off the pot and put it down next to the sheet. And then, they waited.

The mist peeked over the hilltop just as the north wind started to blow and the carrion crows to caw. She carried a salty smell with her, as if she'd been playing with the sea breeze all morning.

She breathed out great puffs, and with each breath, she covered part of the valley. Some afternoons Toletis had seen the mist approach with an especially melancholy air; on those days, she spread out languidly. On other occasions, she would arrive in an organised hurry, covering hilltop after hilltop as if she were an army of trained cotton wool.

Some days, Toletis caught her in a rather playful mood, and she would advance and retreat again and again, ebbing and flowing over the same target until finally deciding to cover it.

From the taste of the air on his tongue, the smell in his nostrils, the caress of the moisture on his face, and the way the mist moved across the valley, Toletis sensed the mood the mist was in every afternoon.

And there were also days when she didn't come. Toletis would ponder the reason for her absence: 'Today she must have woken up a bit achier than normal. She'll be busy with something else today, like preparing more fog for tomorrow's coast.' Or, 'Today she'll have been feeling too lazy to come all the way here.' Or, 'She'll be kneading really thick clouds for the autumn.'

Toletis knew that the mist lived next to the sea, and she was the one that made the clouds in the sky and the froth on the tips of the waves.

He recounted all this to Claudia while they waited for the tender mist to come ashore.

She arrived and mingled readily amongst the hawthorns, the sheet and the pot. This time she was in a good mood, a very good mood.

'Come on, Claudia, hurry, tie a knot over there.'

'Wait a second, Toletis, my pot isn't full ... OK! Now it is! ... Is this alright? Is this how you want the knot?'

'No, maybe slacken it a bit, we don't want to hurt the mist.'

'For goodness sake! Who ever thought the mist would be so fussy?'

'Now bring that corner over here to this one.'

'Wouldn't it have been easier if you'd brought saucepans?'

'How clever! It was almost impossible for me to get the sheet! Can you imagine if I'd asked for a load of pans?'

'Well, I dunno, what about the empty tins from peach slices or chopped tomatoes or roasted red peppers?'

'Don't be such a whiner, Claudia. Can't you see we've got it?'

'Hey, does mist weigh much, Toletis?'

'No. Hold on to it!'

'Wow! That's strange. It doesn't weigh a thing. Not much more than the sheet itself ... same with the pot,' said Claudia, chuckling.

As they walked back, Toletis looked Claudia in the eye very seriously and asked,

'Listen, Claudia, what do you want the mist for? Do you know how to use it?'

'You always think you're so clever. If I don't know how to use it, then I'll learn how to.' Claudia scrunched her face into a little frown and gave her head a little shake.

Toletis wasted no time at all in doling out the mist. He put on some woollen gloves and ran all over the place handing it out:

Patricia was a bleary-eyed kitten with patchy wisps of fur; she weighed 197 grams, and still didn't know how to drink milk from a saucer. She was so weak that she could hardly support her own weight on her hind legs. Her mother had disappeared, and Patricia spent all day whimpering, with her dry, flaky skin and no desire to play or even to find a sunny patch in the farmyard.

A portion of mist put the sparkle back in her eye, and moistened her nose and the tips of her ears. Patricia finally felt safe sitting on her new soft cushion which soothed her rough skin, wiped away her pain and sadness, and softened the feel of the gravel and hay on the pads of her paws. Magically, Patricia suddenly bulked up by 87 grams, and started frisking around and playing with every little thingamabob she found on the ground.

The old stone house was immense and very lonely, forgotten by its owners and at the mercy of the wind and the damp. Cracks had appeared in its façade, and falling tiles had left bare patches on the roof. Its balcony had lost its charm, and the joy had vanished from the faded, wooden-shuttered windows. The house was finding it harder and harder to resist gale-force onslaughts. The wooden panels lining the inside of its ancient walls creaked, and the beams on the ceiling were too weary.

A piece of mist plugged the holes in the roof, fixed up the walls and ceilings, and aired out the inside. The mist shook off the thick layer of dust and gave back the sense of pride that turns a house into a home. The children of the town stopped calling it the witches' house.

The meadows behind Ra's house always had a sombre look to them. Since there were no trees around, the sun beat down hard on the meadows all day, and they never had a chance to recover their green freshness. When they started to improve with the April rain, the cows would turn up and graze away all the best grass.

The meadows always had the droopy appearance of exhaustion. No flowers, no clover; they were patchy, parched and tattered.

A piece of mist put the green back in the grass, and it grew, eager to show off its juicy, emerald radiance, with brightness and pasture for everyone. Cherry, elder and sloe saplings immediately started to sprout in the meadows.

Aunty Anna was bumbling and slow at 107 years old. Hunch-backed and spiritless, her eyes were sunken and tearful. Her long life had melted her nose and ears. With no eyelashes or brows, her face was a map with a million trails where you could read anecdotes of the village fêtes, the first cows that she'd raised with her husband, and the lives of her seven children. Bored and reclusive, half-blind, half-deaf and more than half-living-in-the-past, she didn't expect hardly anything or anyone.

A piece of mist cleared her head and brought back her appetite. Sweet smells surrounded her, and she was filled with a desire to eat. Her skin felt taut, her legs and her back straightened, her cheeks and eyelids filled up, and a gust of life blew up under her skirt right to the crown of her head. Toletis took the last little lump of mist to Ra's apple trees, so that the tower would always feel refreshed.

'That's it. I've run out,' announced Toletis.

'Of all of it?' asked Claudia.

'I mean, I was giving out decent portions. I sorted out the witches' house, which isn't the witches' house any more, and Aunty Anna who doesn't seem so old now, and Patricia, the poor little kitten, who has started jumping around everywhere like a kitten is supposed to. What about you? What did you do with your pot of mist? Don't even think about putting it in the microwave, you'll short the circuit, and we'll end up with burning hot ice-mallows.'

'I'm not stupid, Toletis. I spread it all around my house,' said Claudia, and Toletis understood.

Toletis and Claudia were sitting on the top of the hill next to the hazel trees, looking at the white and red-brown town at the bottom of the valley. Whenever they scaled the hill, things would always get a little bit deep and meaningful. They would only go all the way there, right up to the top, for special occasions, when they had something to say which they deemed truly important. From the hilltop, they had control over the entire valley; they could see enough. No more, no less. Toletis didn't understand why so many grown-ups had an obsession with seeing further and further and further, and with relating the beauty of a mountain with how far you can see from the top of it. He wasn't interested in distant landscapes. The interesting ones were close by, but many people don't appreciate what's close to them, feeling a need to gaze into the distance and the faraway future all the time.

On the hill, they'd seen snakes and fox tracks, lizards of all different colours and strange toadstools that they didn't dare touch. It was the best spot for following the white-tailed kites, and the reflections from Ra's light and the dwindling evening sun. And that hill was where Celemin roamed with his twelve goats, each with its own name and special skill.

People said Celemin was the village idiot, but Claudia and Toletis thought he was the cleverest shepherd in the valley, probably the world. Elsa the goat could imitate the bray of a donkey. Carolina the goat could spin on one hoof. And Lydia the goat could jump to the beat of Celemin's clapping. Celemin had taught them all this!

'You know,' Claudia continued explaining, 'in my house everybody's

always screaming. My Mum and Dad are always shouting. They can't seem to stand each other, and everything ends up in a shrieking match. They jump at any tiny opportunity to boil over and stir up old grudges. They're always in a bad mood, and it's really hard for them to have a conversation without saying something sarcastic, or just going straight for the jugular with criticism and abuse. I'm telling you this, Toletis, but don't tell anyone else. I tipped out some mist in the kitchen, the dining room, and the bedrooms to see if I could lighten the mood at home. I don't know if it'll work. You know I don't really believe that the mist can change things. But this morning, at least, the house was quiet. They both woke up peacefully and didn't get tangled up in one of their silly quarrels; they didn't even argue about what they heard on the radio. Let's see if it lasts until tonight when it's time to decide who's in charge of the TV remote.'

'The mist will come back this afternoon,' is all Toletis said. He was never any good at consoling, even though he felt genuinely sorry about his friends' problems; they affected him a lot. He would think up perfect phrases to cheer somebody up, but then, when it came time to say them, they would get clogged up with saliva. The tone was the hard bit, finding the right tone was what was complicated. So he preferred to stay quiet and give a couple of reassuring pats on the thigh, or a little shoulder squeeze, or a look of complete comprehension. Or, in this case, a little kiss: a kiss close, very close, to Claudia's ear.

'Here's the sheet, Mum. Without any holes,' said Toletis.

'Well, that was quick, wasn't it? Did you get the mist?' asked his mother.

'Yes.'

'And what did you do with it?'

'I fixed the witches' house, which isn't the witches' house anymore. I sorted out Grandad's patchy, parched meadows, and Aunty Anna, and poor little Patricia.'

'And haven't you brought me any?'

'Yes, of course! I brought you a large ball of mist, and you can do what you want with it.'

'And what can I do with it?'

'Um ... you could make air doughnuts, or soap, or a really cool comb, or you could water those gangly geraniums ... or ... or ... Oh! I don't think you'll be doing anything with it.'

'Why not?'

'Because Amenophis has just gulped down the whole thing. Hey! What have you done? That was for Mum! You're a naughty dog.'

Amenophis started to bloat and then to float. His eyes shone more than ever, and his fur fluffed out. His tail looked like a feather duster, as his fringe started to grow.

The poor thing was startled, but he was fine. He floated for three days and three nights, and he had to be tied to the leg of the heaviest table so that he didn't go up too high. They had to climb up on a stepping-stool to feed him, and when he tried to bark, all that came out was a howl. His belly was rounder than round, and his ears pointed up weirdly.

When the mist wore off, he began to run around and bark as if he were drunk, but he soon went back to being lazy old Amenophis.

'Next time I go back up the hill, Mum, I'll bring you the tastiest, chunkiest, ripest hazelnuts in the world,' promised Toletis, to make up for the lost ball of mist.

3

Spring

THE WOBBEGONG LANGUAGE

'Toletis … Next time, please write your essay in English!'

Miss Montse looked at him over the top of her teacher's glasses, as she scowled and said nothing more.

It was June. The academic year was coming to a close, and Toletis had failed languages. He knew perfectly well why. The Wobbegongs were to blame.

He had always had an affinity with Miss Montse, but now she was starting to grind him down because she didn't understand him or make even the slightest effort to try and do so.

Miss Montse was tall and skinny. She had a treacle sweet voice and always wore lilac or pink espadrilles, even in winter, even if it was snowing. As soon as it started to get just a little warmer, she would put on sleeveless tops.

Miss Montse was thirty-none years old. Toletis always used to say that number, because in reality he didn't know how old she was. She never wanted to say, and she never celebrated her birthday at school; she didn't even bring in any sweeties or lollipops or anything. She only liked celebrating Saint David's Day, on 1st March, because it marked the end of the coldest and darkest days, and announced spring's imminent arrival. On that date, she would bring delicious little chocolates in the shape of dragons; she made them herself with a mould that she said she had bought on a trip to Wales.

She had always given Toletis good grades, so the fail had not gone down well at all.

Toletis had always been very advanced in languages. He enjoyed playing word games by comparing words that were almost the same, but had very different meanings: amused and bemused, bountiful and bounceable, bazaar and bizarre, dingy and dinghy. 'Imagine you said: what a bounceable vegetable patch my grandfather has. It would be an absolute load of codswallop, Tutan. And it's very easy to fall into that trap,' he taught his friend. He also liked to linger on the sounds in especially playful words, like she-nanigans, nincom-poop, repeti-ti-ti-tive.

He loved reading encyclopaedias and dictionaries page by page, as if they were novels. What's more, one of his greatest pastimes was playfully building sentences that seemed to be totally fine, but were actually impossible and meaningless. He would then put his inventions to Tutan so that he could try to guess whether they were possible or not. 'It's not worth it anymore, it's already too soon,' was one of his favourite impossible sentences. And this one, 'It couldn't have happened, it's already late.'

But the Wobbegong language that he'd learnt from his buxom Aunty Josefina was making his life tough.

This is the Wobbegong language. Its vocabulary is made up of 47 words. Some of them are words we all know, some exist only for Toletis and his Aunty Josefina:

Wobbegong. Bumblewee. Busybody. Brittlebit. Barbecue. Bellboy.

Balderdash. Rubylocks. Bilibate. Batfish. Dodgy-bodger. Bubblesome.

Discombobulate. Caboose. Bludger. Blubbery. Bullocking.

Thingamabobble. Booby. Babirusa. Bumboat. Squibble. Nobble. Wibble. Bibble.

Collywobbler. Quibsnib. Gobbledygook. Blubby.

Underbelly. Smellybutton. Flabby. Feeble. Nibbly. Mamba.

Blubberbus. Blunderbuss. Bubblegum. Blobbytum.

Kebabble. Frobscottle. Flibbertigibbet. Bobbly. Babble. Belfry. Bellicose and Bellington Woots.

'He made such a blubby mess, even the wobbegong got up and left. Look at that girl, she's a total collywobbler. What a bunch of bludgers, they live in a right old caboose. He's a dodgy-bodger. And what a squibbly bunch his kids are. He always wibbles when he nibbles, but at least while he's eating, he's not babbling so much piffle. Stop picking bobbles from your smellybutton, get in the shower and scrub your blobbytum. He seems like a bit of a bobbly bumboat to me. He's grumbling like a babirusa. I'm telling you, that man's got batfish in the belfry.'

That's how Aunty Josefina spoke, with her semi-invented vocabulary full of the letter "b" and, above all, with a bubbling, burbling sound. It was, without a doubt, not very grammatical, but it was fun and very expressive.

'Don't be a busybody, or a flibbertigibbet, or a discombobulater. You ought to be respectabable and honourabable,' is what she used to say to Toletis. And, even though she never explained those words to him, he knew perfectly well, because of the way they sounded, what his Aunty was implying.

That way of speaking was contagious, and Toletis picked it up just like you pick up Scottish, Welsh or Irish accents if you hear them for long enough at a time. And he started to converse with his Aunty Josefina with her feeble billycans, barbecued beefcakes, rubylocks, frobscottles, and kebabbles.

So, the words, rather than being formed of syllables, were composed of syllabubbles.

Toletis found he was comfortable with that language, and he considered re-baptising himself as Bubba, Beda or Biscop after the Anglo-Saxon Kings of Lindsey, which chimed well with the musicality of his vocabulary. But in the end, he decided to keep the Egyptian nickname and leave Bubba-da-Biscop for special occasions, and only ever as a middle name.

Tutankhamun the polyglot had also had a bad time with Miss Montse. He'd sometimes mix up all the languages in his head and would reply in class with a bark or a growl. Miss Montse, of course, thought he was trying to make fun of her, and as soon as she started to scowl,

Tutan would realise he'd made a mistake, try to rectify it, and go back to speaking with human words.

But he was the cleverest in class, so Miss Montse would always forgive him straight away.

At least he didn't get mixed up in written exams, because it's very difficult, almost impossible, to get most animal sounds onto paper. For example, how on earth do you write down the hellos of a swallow?

Tutankhamun also wanted to be shown the ways of the Wobbegong language. Accustomed as he was to the language of grasshoppers and rooks, he picked up Aunty Josefina's in an instant. With a few lessons like these: 'Even the wobbegong's left means things are every which way. A dodgy-bodger is somebody who doesn't put any effort into what they're doing. If you're dodgy-bodging, you'll try not to do something, and when you're forced to do it, you'll do it badly. A thingamabobble is a thingamajig, a muddle, or codswallop. A bubblesome person is a buoyant, lively person with panache and a cheeky sense of humour. Babirusa is an affectionate term. And kebabble is what comes out if somebody tries to speak while eating a kebab.'

Toletis Bubba-da-Biscop even gave his friend homework so that he could keep advancing his new language skills. He had to fill in the blanks in unfinished sentences using the right words from the Wobbegong vocabulary.

Of course, Aunty Josefina didn't realise she was doing anything odd. She used all these terms as if it were the most natural thing in the world,

as if they'd always been in all the English dictionaries. Toletis's family weren't worried when the boy spoke Wobbegong, because they were used to hearing Aunty Josefina. Only Claudia, who did everything very conscientiously, had warned Toletis that by using those nouns and verbs, he'd eventually end up forgetting the words everybody else was using.

Miss Montse decided to give Toletis a second chance, and a week later, she gave him another language exam to see if he'd pass the subject. In the second exam, he was more careful, and he passed. From then on, he saved his Aunty Josefina's language for speaking to the mist, to his Grandfather Ra, and to the tower of trees; for playing with Tutan; and for those grand occasions when he would climb to the hilltop with Claudia. And, of course, he used it to talk to his Aunty Josefina.

He did save it for one other thing.

After that month of June, Toletis started writing stories and poems in the Wobbegong language. Poems like this one:

> The flabby babirusa had a wibbly underbelly,
> He always combed his rubylocks and shared his bubblegum,
> But he invited such a rabble to his famous barbecue,
> And the biggest meanest collywobbler poked his blobbytum
> But the rabble all kebabbled while the babirusa blubbed,

Or this one:

Add a blubbery nobble to the cauldron of frobscottle,

And don't forget a drop of bumblewee,

'Cos when the mamba and the bellboy come over for a bottle,

They'll discombobulate the booby and his friend the BFG.

At the start of every poem or story he would also insert the Wobbegong vocabulary, and at the end, he would write notes in the form of a game and a learning exercise for whoever read it:

'Which words from the Wobbegong dictionary have been used on this occasion? Make sentences with those words using them properly.'

Oh! And naturally, his poems were always signed by Toletis Bubba-da-Biscop, with a curly flourish swooping over the signature and a smile underneath.

4

Summer

ALEXANDER ATHERTON—AITKEN

Tutankhamun had a slightly strange perspective. Instead of blinking at a millisecond rate like everybody else, which is hardly noticeable and doesn't hinder normal vision, his eyes would close for two seconds every time he lowered his eyelids. Because of this, Tutan had a dozy appearance and a peculiar way of looking at everything. He tended to reflect on things, and enjoyed contemplating scenery and beautiful people and lots of interesting objects much more than other kids, simply because he had less time to see them.

But that summer, Tutankhamun was raising his eyelids even slower because Alexander Atherton-Aitken was making him very nervous. That boy had been brought up in the city and had never been to a small town, and as soon as he set foot in Toletis's valley for a two-week holiday in Claudia's parents' farmhouse, the first thing that came to his head and his mouth was the question: 'Is this some kind of farm-school?'

'Umm, no. This is a town, and we live here all year quite marvellously, thank you very much,' responded Claudia firmly.

The day after Alexander Atherton-Aitken arrived, Toletis, Claudia, Tutan and Amenophis decided to have a meeting on the hilltop.

'Great! We've got a nightmare summer in store,' Claudia blurted out. 'And do we have to call him Alexander Atherton-Aitken?' she added.

'It's so long,' Tutan piped up.

'And just using the vowels is an ordeal,' said Toletis. 'It'd be Aeaeaeoaie.   Impossible.'

'Impossible,' agreed Claudia.

'Well, I might just call him "A-A-A,"' Toletis decided.

'Among us, so we understand each other, that's not a bad idea. We'll call him A-A-A, okay?' Tutan concluded.

Alexander Atherton-Aitken had never seen nettles. And when he was next to some, he asked:

'Do you use these plants to concoct some kind of medicinal herbal tea?'

'I wouldn't touch them,' Toletis warned him. 'And, if you do, hold your breath. If you don't, you'll come out in super-itchy hives.'

'Rubbish! That's just a superstition.'

'Go on then.'

And on he went. Righteously. And along came the tears. But he'd learnt his lesson.

He was scared of the cows, having got them confused with the bulls he'd heard would charge anything red. Toletis, Claudia and Tutan did everything they could to get him to go over to an innocent little calf. Nope, impossible. They failed.

'Can't you see how they're looking at me?' asked the fearful Alexander Atherton-Aitken.

'It's only curiosity. You're a novelty. Cows are very curious, and they gaze intently. And with those huge eyes, it's as if they're staring even more seriously, but they're not planning anything evil,' explained Toletis.

He wasn't allowed to touch dogs, because his Mum had told him that they were 'transmitters of so many diseases.' So there was no way he'd play with Amenophis.

In the stables, he'd tiptoe around. 'It's disgusting in here. Let's not hang around, or I'll get my shoes dirty,' he would protest as soon as they went into one. There was no way he was going to get to know the pigs in the sties, or distinguish the smell of a cow-pat from a sheep poo pellet, skills that Toletis had picked up when he was barely five years old.

Whenever he sat on the grass, he'd whinge about the ants. Out in the pastures, he'd moan about the horseflies, and in the houses, he'd whine about the flies. 'They must sell all types of products in the corner shop to kill these bugs,' he would snap to Toletis's neighbours whenever the chance arose. And he would go on to inform them that, 'Insects are the main vectors of the contagious diseases that have done the most damage to Humanity.'

But, what annoyed Toletis, Claudia and Tutan the most was that Alexander Atherton-Aitken didn't notice the verdant tower of Ra's apple trees or the house that was always misty.

'A-A-A is pretty thick. Much dumber than Celemin, despite what everyone else says,' decided Claudia after a few days. 'Yesterday, Toletis, A-A-A told me that he couldn't believe your parents hadn't taken you to the doctor to have your ears pinned back, like other kids go and get braces on their teeth to straighten them. I told him that your parents always wanted a pet rabbit, and that now that you've got the ears, they're going to get you braces for your teeth, but to push them out, not to pull

them in. You'll look like you have a snout, and then you'll be well on your way to being a bunny.'

Claudia and Tutan laughed a lot, but Toletis remained a little lost in thought. Claudia was using A-A-A's story to make fun of him. Toletis quickly decided that he didn't mind, and in the end, he was chortling, too.

Alexander Atherton-Aitken never believed Tutan could talk to animals or that Celemin's goats knew how to heehaw and dance; and he also thought it was absurd that the boys could tell where Claudia had been simply by smelling her hair.

'You just want to wind me up and trick me,' he commented one day in all seriousness. 'But, you should know that, according to all my teachers, I'm a very bright boy, and I take everything on board quickly and easily. E-ver-y-thing.'

Alexander Atherton-Aitken always won the games on his smartphone. However, he always came last in the Sounds-of-Silence game.

Clear August evenings when the mist stayed away, Toletis, Claudia and Tutankhamun were in the habit of climbing the bell tower to play a game where they had to find hidden sounds.

As the light dwindled, silence would spread across the town. If you focused and stayed very still, avoided making even the tiniest noise of swallowing, you'd start noticing the sounds of the countryside. They were so well intermingled that at first they gave the impression of silence.

Scanning the empty airwaves, the three children would put a soundtrack to the evening thicket by identifying the bumbling of the bees and other insects, the insistent song of the crickets, and the rustle of the poplar leaves in even the lightest of breezes. Often the extremely zealous chirping and twittering of the nightingales and robins, or the kwawaa brip-bip-bip of a quail, would take centre stage.

Tutan specialised in investigating the clinking of cowbells in the air, and Claudia was a master of warning about the inopportune arrival of mosquitos, not only from their buzzing but because she would also get covered in goose pimples.

And Toletis never missed a harrier: neither the jump-jets that sometimes scored the valley sky with a distant roar (Toletis thought every plane was a jump-jet, since how else could a plane take off inside a valley?), nor the rare hen harriers whose shrieks accompanied sweeping food passes and sky-dances.

A-A-A looked on perplexed.

'Yeah, right. You're all just pulling my leg. You can't hear all that.'

A 'sshhhh!' would hush him.

There was more. Everything reached the belfry: the crows cawing and the dogs barking and the calves softly mooing, the odd human voice chattering with the dairy cattle during milking, and the last orange-violet rays of the sun. Yes, the sun's rays, because Claudia was adamant that those final glimmers as each day closed sounded something like the finest violins. But Tutan and Toletis never managed to hear them, and they were convinced Claudia had just imagined the sound of violins. And it's best not to even mention what A-A-A thought!

'I'm going back to the farmhouse; I can't put up with you lot anymore … Saying that the sunset sounds like violins. I'm going to go home and put on some Beethoven. That sounds like violins, not this nonsense. Claudia, you've gone completely hurdy-gurdy … '

'I've gone hurdy-gurdy!' Claudia laughed. 'Did he just say I've gone hurdy-gurdy?!'

That night, the Sounds-of-Silence game ended in enormous guffaws.

The truth is Claudia, Toletis and Tutan ended up having fun with A-A-A. The valley was different with him. It was full of risks and dangers, and even the simplest everyday task turned into something totally new: a challenge, an adventure. There was more pleasure to be had, and they inflated everything with their imaginations in order to further bewilder the incredulous and cowardly A-A-A.

Gathering the eggs every afternoon that the hens had laid amongst the hay in the barns became a detective novel. 'You have to sniff each piece of hay and every last nook. When it smells like chicks, it means we're near the nest,' Toletis whispered to A-A-A, as if it were top secret information.

They invented terrifying legends for every corner of the town. One day, near a patch of dry grass in a meadow, they spun this tale: 'See that? It's the grave of a donkey that died from eating too many carrots. Ever since its death, grass will not grow here. And if anybody dares to cross that patch while eating carrots, the very ground itself brays a heehaw from the earthy depths that'll give you goose bumps all over and make every single hair stand on end.'

Claudia, of course, was perfectly poised to embellish her theory of the curse of the dogs with various speculations. She couldn't help it. When she looked deep into a dog's sad eyes, she always came to the same conclusion: 'They're people suffering under some kind of spell, and when they look at us like that, they're trying to show their misfortune, beseeching us to, please, do something, because they're tired of walking on all fours, barking, and eating bones and dog food.'

Claudia was staunchly committed to her theory, and never passed up any little chance to gaze attentively at a dog and touch its ears; she said that she would keep on doing it until a dog turned into a perceptive young man, a fairy-tale friend who would want to explore 77 valleys with her.

A-A-A always shot down the stories they told him with the same phrase: 'That's just not rational.' But the truth is that he swallowed all the stories despite his protestations.

The ideal time for their imaginations to soar was when the mist drew near. Toletis, emboldened by his vaporous friend, invented one very peculiar story: 'On some days, the mist is especially insatiable, and it snatches the smallest children in the town. It takes them to the mountain

caves to be raised by wolves so the race of wild hairy people that live in the forests along with the roe deer, roebucks and warthogs don't die out. They can't read or write, but they have a special skill for understanding nature, making soup from moss, and concocting medicines from the woodland toadstools. To show their gratitude, the wolves sing to the mist. That's the howling you can hear when the moon is full.'

But what really turned A-A-A's blood to curds and whey were the toads. And to make matters worse, Tutan had added his own inventive twist to A-A-A's disgust:

'Toletis's Grandfather told me that if there's a really strong summer storm and it pours with rain, toads lose their fear of people and decide to go into houses looking for the one thing that can stop them from being so ugly: a little bit of aniseed. If a toad gets hold of just a couple of drops of ouzo, it changes completely and becomes a little bright blue bird, a bit like a hummingbird with a very, very thin beak. But this has to happen during a seriously heavy summer storm, because if not, the drink does nothing and they remain the same slimy, warty toads as before.'

With A-A-A the valley turned into a world teeming with enchantments and monsters, good animals and evil beasts, gigantic hilltop castles, and puddles that had once been oceans and had shrunk all of a sudden.

A-A-A had learnt quickly, and not just about the logical and simple side of life: that nettles sting, that cows are very curious, and that if you sit on the grass it's very likely some ants will appear. He had also learnt about all the wonders that are hidden in a valley, if you know how to look for them.

5

Summer

THE LIAN

On his last day before going back to the city, A-A-A surprised his friends by narrating a fantastical story to them. It was the story of The Lian; and Claudia, Toletis and Tutan never forgot it, and occasionally, mostly when up on the hill, they would take turns recounting the story out loud so that the memory of it would never be consigned to the abyss.

This is how A-A-A told it:

'You see that house you used to call the witches' house, and now it's the misty house? That's where The Lian lived.

Julian was hopelessly struck by fear when war broke out in this area. He heard on the radio that the fighting had started, and he didn't wait around for the bombs and gunshots to reach his town. He searched around for a decent hidey-hole, and when he couldn't find what he wanted, he dug a cave under one of the troughs in his pigpen. He grabbed some things to eat, plus several bottles of water and wine, and he climbed in. He lived all alone and nobody knew anything about his plan. In the town, all his neighbours thought he'd gone away to fight in the war.

Days and weeks passed, and Julian stayed hidden in his cave that was a little over seven times bigger than his body.

As his food and drink reserves ran out, Julian started to go out some nights when everybody was sleeping. He would head for people's vegetable patches and wheelie bins to see if he could find something to nibble on; and he'd fill up a big jug of water from the spring. Before the first rays of light peeked over the horizon, he would climb back into his hidey-hole under the trough.

Julian didn't speak to anybody. His radio ran out of batteries, so when the war ended, Julian didn't hear the news. When he didn't reappear, everybody in the valley thought he had died in battle. They added his name to the list carved into the great cross that was erected in the town square. Yet he remained in hiding. One year passed, then another, then another: three whole years. But he couldn't shake off his fear; he didn't want the war to find him.

Over time, his nocturnal escapades became more frequent. Until, one day, three kids from the town, who had crept out of their houses in the middle of the night so they could go and water some trees on the hill with fizzy water, saw him in the distance. They tracked him and watched him step into the abandoned house, the house that was said to be inhabited only by witches.

Little by little, piecing together what they'd seen with what the grown-ups were saying, the children began to concoct the fantastic story of The Lian, mixing the name of that man with "lion" to get a word that perfectly fit the magical and mysterious being.

The children even invented playful songs based on The Lian's myths. Songs like this one: "He only goes out by night, he eats what he finds in the bins, his beard is three yards long, and it really, really stinks. Who is it? Who is it? Who is it? ... It's The Lian!"

The legend gradually spread around the town. But nobody – neither old nor young – ever dared go into the house.

If Julian really was The Lian, the townsfolk respected his metamorphosis. Many neighbours even threw away whole bloomers of bread or chunks of ham or ripe apples so that The Lian could thrive. He, on the other hand, noticed one day that some youngsters were spying on him from behind a garden wall, so he stopped going out so often, and when he did go out, it was even later at night and more cautiously.

Nobody could ever prove whether the loaves of bread and the ripe apples from the rubbish were being eaten by foxes or by The Lian. It was only over time, fifteen years after the end of the war, that people noticed nobody was eating the food anymore.

The house is still there, more crumbly and forgotten by the day. Nobody has ever gone back in there, and nobody knows what is in there. One day, a generous-hearted boy filled it with mist, but I'm telling you:

Don't ever go inside; don't ever go in there, guys, because they say that The Lian still lives there and that now he survives on whatever is brought to him by the witches disguised as black cats. If a curious kid should happen to enter the house, no one knows how The Lian would react. He might go berserk when he realises that he's been discovered, thinking the soldiers will soon be there to drag him away.'

They told that story so many times, sitting together on the hilltop, that Claudia, Toletis and Tutankhamun ended up believing it. Convinced it was true, every time they walked past Julian's house, they would fondly remember A-A-A, that city boy who would go everywhere with his smartphone and who in the beginning seemed so weird to them. All three of them would say:

'Don't ever go in there. Don't ever go in there, guys, because The Lian might go crazy.'

'And what if we do go in?' Claudia asked once, intrigued, opening her eyes widely to convey her fascination to Toletis, Tutan and Amenophis.

The first to react was Amenophis, who let out a long, loud howl.

Next was Tutan, who started to blink even more slowly. This always happened when he was nervous. It was a strange reaction, but that's what he did.

And finally, Toletis. You didn't have to be very observant to notice that his ears had stretched upwards and grown even pointier. When it came to answering her, the order was reversed.

First, Toletis. He said, 'Okay.'

Then, Tutan. He said, 'Okay.'

And then, Amenophis. He said, 'Grrrrruff!' which in dog language, according to Tutan's translation, means 'okay' when the 'R' is rolled and the 'U' is very short.

In truth, the four of them had been waiting for a moment like this to enter the witches' house, the house of mist, or Julian's or The Lian's house: all names which had been given to the most mysterious house in town.

They didn't wait another moment, because all four of them knew that if they left it for another day, then it would prey on their minds, and in the end, the dread would creep up from their toes and stop them in their tracks.

It was getting dark – that dusky twilight when the sun has almost set, but not quite. Toletis grabbed a torch. Claudia brought a tambourine from home, asserting that it was the best way to scare away witches in case any came out. Tutan brought an apple to throw to the Lian, lest he still be alive.

The four headed off. The house was open, and they only had to push the door gently. The hinges made a deep, grating sound.

And then …

They went in.

They parted the mist with their hands, as if it were a giant curtain, and they carefully shone the torch to be sure about where they were stepping. Amenophis was sniffing everything.

There were, in fact, witches. The children started to see donkeys eating carrots, princes with snouts, barking as if they were dogs, and a kind of hummingbird-toad that flapped around in a state of panic.

All of their imaginative visions, all the tales they'd told to A-A-A that summer were in the house.

Claudia was the only one who spoke – and just this: 'Woah! This is cool!'

It was cold, and they were shivering and on the verge of fainting. But it was Amenophis who was the bravest and most steadfast. He used

his canines to grab their trousers one by one and drag them out into the fresh evening air without wasting another moment in there.

Amenophis saw that the kids were going crazy, and he wasn't going to stand by and watch it happen. A couple of firm growls and barks once he'd dragged them all out. Sorted! Full stop! And grr, grr, grrrruuaauff, which, in dog language, means, 'Come on. There's nothing to see here.'

6

Summer

PAINTED LANDSCAPES

On August afternoons when the mist stayed away, Matthias would venture out to paint his valley landscapes.

It was only on those afternoons when the heat was bearable and only in that month – August – because Matthias wasn't interested in capturing any other lights and colours in his paintings. He liked those golden, slightly violet summertime hues. And he was such a perfectionist that he'd spent the last seven summers adding tiny brushstrokes to his landscapes: little dots of colour, painstakingly applied.

Matthias was one of those special people with pizzazz; he had pale, smooth skin, blue eyes, and hair with flecks of copper tied into a ponytail. Two swallows fluttered around his russet locks, making him even more intriguing to the children. The birds never left him.

Toletis was slightly annoyed that Matthias appealed so much to Claudia. Toletis was jealous. He couldn't avoid it no matter how much he repeated time and again that Matthias was a cool guy and that only a fool would be suspicious of him.

Those August evenings when the mist was otherwise occupied and they chose not to play the Sounds-of-Silence game, Toletis, Claudia and Tutankhamun usually headed up to the spot on the hillside where Matthias, squinting with concentration, would be adding strokes and colours to his works of art.

They would see how, little by little – ever so little by little – things would appear on the canvas: green shrubs, blue mountains in the distance, red-tiled roofs and white-washed facades, dry-stone walls and dry, gnarled elms, the tower of Ra's apple trees, and the rows of hazel trees along the ridge of hilltops.

Sunbeams peeking over the horizon gave the scenery depth and perspective, as the shafts of light and elongated shadows danced amongst the gently rolling meadows of freshly cut hay.

If they had to keep quiet during the Sounds-of-Silence game, going to see Matthias was no different. The painter was so focussed on the task at hand that it seemed like he was trying to use his paintbrush not only to apply colours, but sounds and smells as well.

The three children and the painter hardly exchanged any words. The kids would say hello by raising their eyebrows, and Matthias would respond with an affectionate wink.

Later, at home, Toletis would practise his winking in the mirror to see if he could get it to come out looking as charming as Matthias's, accompanied with a half-smile and the slightest dimple in his cheek. But his was a disaster. In light of his failures, he persevered with practising his eyebrow raise, despite his negative feelings about it. He thought it was a much sillier gesture, whilst the wink had a proven twinkly effect on Claudia.

After one of their visits to see the painter, Claudia, Tutan and Toletis delved into an artistic critique. Well, 'artistic' in their terms.

'I think he should paint a bit of sea,' suggested Claudia.

'Duh! Have you gone completely loopy? You can't see the sea from this valley, even if you climb the highest mountain,' Toletis remarked.

'Claudia, can't you see that Matthias is a realist painter?' added Tutan, the know-it-all, 'And, if he's a realist, he has to paint what he sees, he can't invent stuff.'

'But the picture would be better with a nice big patch of turquoise sea; you can't deny it,' insisted Claudia.

'She's lost it! Why do you want the sea so badly, when all it does is make you seasick?' interjected Toletis.

'Anyway, I don't see why he can't invent anything. Haven't you seen the pictures in our textbooks? Joan Miró invented everything, those yellow circles, blue lines and red spirals. They looked pretty cool, and he's really famous,' she explained in an excited rush.

'But, look, if he paints a sea into the picture, he wouldn't be able to fit in those huge meadows that look so great,' argued Toletis. 'And, why do you want the sea anyway, Claudia, when the water is always so freezing?'

'It makes no difference, smarty-pants, and you are a smarty-pants. It would never occur to me to take a swim in one of Matthias's paintings; I just think it would be prettier,' Claudia retorted, 'and then he could put in some seagulls. They always make a painting much more beautiful.'

'But he's already painted swallows and swifts. That's why they're always flying around with him,' added Tutan.

'The painting seems a bit gloomy to me. I can't help it! Some waves, a few seagulls and a couple of fishing boats would liven it up, for sure!' Claudia went on.

'Boats as well?' asked a bewildered Toletis.

'Sure. And then he could paint some fishermen smoking a pipe on the shore and some women casting the nets, and some children playing with lobster pots. And a sailing boat on the horizon,' concluded Claudia.

'But, Claudia, can't you see that's got nothing to do with our valley?' erupted Toletis, reining in her unrestrained imagination.

Another day, Claudia told them about how she'd prefer a snowy landscape even though Matthias only painted in the middle of August. And on one occasion, she suggested sprinkling the fields with shepherds' shacks. Another time, she thought it would be a good idea to cover the hilltop with medieval castles and towers.

In reality, what Claudia was doing was pulling Tutankhamun and Toletis's legs, but the two boys took all her ideas very seriously.

Later that summer, watching Matthias apply pigments to canvas, the silence was suddenly broken by the artist,

'Come on, I'll show it to you.'

Matthias was about to fulfil his promise, postponed 77 times, of showing them his studio where he stored all his brushes, paints and canvases.

Claudia was so nervous that she didn't say a word, and little hairs started to ping off her head like sparks because she was so excited.

When Matthias saw this, he let out a fanfare of laughter. He picked up his stuff, folded his easel, carefully packed away his little tubes of

paint, and declared, 'Let's go!'

On the way there, Toletis's eyes began to sparkle brighter and brighter. Claudia tripped over every rock along the pathway, and Tutan blinked yet more slowly.

They went into Matthias's house. Up one flight of stairs, then another. On the third floor, in a loft with an enormous skylight: the world of the painter.

None of them had imagined it would be like this.

It was like the Sounds-of-Silence game. At first sight, there didn't seem to be anything, except bright white walls, a stream of light, a massive chunk of sky in the roof, and blank sheets and canvases.

But when they looked closer at the whiteness, they discovered the most fascinating objects. Claudia, who had hardly opened her mouth from nerves, let out a scream and shouted: 'Look!'

Matthias released another symphony of laughter, this time so loud that it spooked the swallows around his head a little and they started to flutter even more skittishly. Claudia was pointing at the half-hunched skeleton of a bird, which was staring straight up from between a small bundle of white papers.

Matthias explained that he'd found it in the attic while clearing things out for his studio, and he decided to keep it in case one day he felt like painting it. He told them that it was a kestrel that had been shot.

Tutan didn't scream, but his face did distort into Tutan-Come-on-let's-get-out-of-here! He had just seen a couple of really thick snakes preserved in a jar of alcohol. Matthias said that he'd also found them in the old attic, covered in spider webs, and that he didn't really want to paint them, and if anybody wanted them, they could have them. All three shook their heads rapidly, rejecting the offer; and just so there was no doubt, they vocalised it: No, no, no, no, no, no, no thanks.

Toletis's gaze fell on the incredible light show that a group of glass jars, bottles and vases was projecting onto a white surface, creating a rainbow. He imagined a village of gnomes living there, amongst the reflections in the glass, whose mission was to polish the rays of light so that they would shine even brighter.

It smelled like paint and practically nothing else, perhaps a hint of flowers and dry herbs. Yes, in fact, in an old glass sugar bowl there was a mixture of camomile, lavender and rosemary.

It was amazing to be able to go around discovering details about the painter's life hidden amidst the bareness of the room: from the kestrel's skeleton and the jars of snakes, to the glass village of gnomes and the sugar bowl of camomile. Claudia, who by now had grown more confident, was twirling around as if spellbound. And Toletis noticed how the jealousy started to well up in his toes and was about to reach his knees.

Rummaging around in the whiteness, however, it was impossible to find any painted landscapes.

'But, where are all the paintings?' asked Toletis, who could no longer hold back his curiosity.

'They are here, but they're facing the wall,' replied Matthias after some loud and hearty laughter, and he started to turn round the canvases.

The three children were struck dumb and frozen to the spot. All the pictures were the same landscape; the same valley ... but different. The more of his works Matthias revealed, the more speechless and immobile they became. The painter's landscapes had, unknowingly, soaked in lots of Claudia's ideas. On seeing this, Claudia's head started to give off so many little sparky hairs that Toletis thought, for a moment, she might end up bald.

There was one landscape with a snow-covered valley, and a valley with castles on the hill, and a valley with a sprinkling of shepherds' shacks, and a valley with a bit of sea with little boats.

Toletis looked over at Claudia and decided that she must have known all along, that she'd already been to the studio, and that the whole time she'd been teasing him and Tutan. He wanted to disappear in a puff of smoke, to turn invisible. He wanted to spirit himself away. Moments like this made him feel so terrible that he would have liked to have been able to utter a magic word and be shot from a magic cannon to land somewhere far away. He had a crushing tummy ache and a weight on his chest.

Claudia realised straight away what was going on. She looked deeply into Toletis's eyes and told him very calmly,

'I didn't know a thing. Honestly, Toletis, I had no idea. I promise you.' She was in so much shock that she struggled to get the sounds together to form the words.

Matthias chuckled again when he saw the state they were in, and he tousled each one's hair in turn, as if to bring them back to reality.

'So, do you like them?' he asked.

And all three, as if they had come to an agreement, said slowly and at the same time: 'Yes, of course,' to which Claudia added, with an emphasis on each syllable, 'they are Ay … May … Zing!'

There was something else that caught Toletis's eye and helped him get over his queasy feeling.

None of the paintings were finished. Not a single landscape had received all of its brushstrokes, all of its shades, all of its colours. No picture was complete. All of them had blank spaces, holes that would draw your gaze, bottomless pits that the lines and shapes were scampering into. Nothing was perfect or complete in the artist's life. Everything was open, like the giant skylight in the ceiling.

And Matthias himself left every autumn to go to distant lands – some said Iceland, others Denmark – and he wouldn't come back until the following summer, and for that whole time nobody in the valley knew anything about the ethereal painter. And so it was with each painting, which reached a point where it would get lost and disappear, and stop telling its story.

Matthias noticed that the children were staring at the blank spots. Another of his chortles burst out, but all he said was:

'That way nobody buys them, and I get to keep them forever.'

Toletis thought about the lovely things in his life – his Mum and Claudia, Tutan and Amenophis, his valley with the evening sunlight and the mist, his box of photos, Ra's tower, and Sunday mornings. And he spent time ruminating on the idea of always leaving a little secret, intimate, blank, unrevealed gap so that nobody could snatch away those things that meant so much to him, so that they would always be close to him.

7

Autumn

HAZELNUTS FOR MUM

'Next time I go back up the hill, Mum, I'll bring you the tastiest, chunkiest, ripest hazelnuts in the world.'

The time had come.

Toletis had a promise to keep and could only do so during those days when summer melds into autumn, when the sun sets much earlier and the sky doesn't shine quite as brightly at midday.

He asked Claudia if she would accompany him. And the two of them and Amenophis headed off to the hills, stopping every so often to pick sage for Granny Ursula's sausages, and blackberries and bilberries for Auntie Josefina's jams; or dropping everything to watch a strange blue or purple butterfly, or to pull out the weeds from around a small willow tree standing out amongst the sedge.

Claudia and Toletis took a snack with them – salami sandwiches and some bananas and peaches – as well as a couple of sturdy sticks to help with the uphill climb.

Toletis's Mum had warned them not to come back down too late: 'You can't see anything at night, and the path becomes much more dangerous. It's very stony and you could trip and fall.' Toletis's Mum worried a lot about accidents out in nature.

His Dad was pretty different. He wasn't afraid of anything; he was so strong that he could stop a cow in its tracks with his bare hands.

Toletis hardly ever saw his Dad who spent all day on the tractor. He worked from sunrise to sunset making hay, fertilising the soil, planting potatoes or harvesting them, taking the cows to the mountain pastures

or bringing them back, weeding the vegetables or travelling from one cattle fair to another to trade his calves.

There were plenty of days when the relationship between Toletis and his father was whittled down to watching the news together in the morning and a goodnight kiss before bedtime.

Toletis liked his Dad's back. It was so broad, his shoulders so solid and his hands so huge. He hadn't seen his Dad's legs since he was a young toddler. His Dad never wore swimming trunks or shorts, and his tweed-wearing sense of modesty meant he wouldn't let anybody see him in his underpants. Toletis abounded with curiosity. He longed to see his Dad's legs to check if they were the same as his.

Before starting their search for the tastiest, ripest hazelnuts on the hill, Claudia and Toletis sat down to eat their snacks and discuss the important things they had been through over the past few days. Amenophis entertained himself by stalking some flies and grasshoppers.

Claudia's hair smelled of green beans. Every afternoon Toletis knew what Claudia had eaten from the smell of her hair. It didn't matter if it was lentils or macaroni or rice or green beans, he could smell it. He also found it easy to guess where his friend had been, whether she'd walked past any lavender or through meadows of long dry grass.

Claudia's hair was like a sponge and a weathervane. With a bit of practice, just by looking at it and touching it, you'd know the temperature and humidity levels perfectly well. You could also tell which season it was, because the colour changed according to the amount of sunlight, and it went from almost black in winter to very light chestnut in summer. From checking the curliness, you could tell what mood she was in, too. On days when she was sad, because of quarrels at home, she would appear with limp, straight hair, but when she was cheerful and calm her hair would turn a bit wavy. If she felt scared or nervous, her hair would stand on end a little, and if she felt tired, her shoulders would be full of hair that had fallen out.

Claudia confessed to Toletis that she couldn't stand Christopher Columbus. She thought he was an arrogant so-and-so who not only treated the Native Americans badly, but his own sailors as well. She was worried because it was what they were studying in the second term at school, and it was one of the most important lessons in the history textbook that year, and she couldn't even get through the first page. And the picture of the conquistador didn't do him any favours: with a fox fur drooping over his shoulders, his beady lying eyes, and a hairstyle and hat that gave him a smarmy air.

Toletis told Claudia about his huge issue that week. That Sunday he had to go and visit his Dad's family, and he was really dreading it. He knew what they were going to say to him and to his parents, 'Don't you eat enough? You're all skin and bones. You have to eat well to grow into a strong lad.' 'His ears are sticking out more and more. Shouldn't you take him to see a doctor?' 'How are your grades? Are you passing all your exams? You have to apply yourself now, or you'll never get ahead in the world.' And then, they'd cap it off with a ridiculous wink and a nudge in the ribs: 'So … have you got your eye on any girls back home?'

It was always the same. They never asked him what games he'd been playing that summer, or how Patricia the kitten was, or whether he got annoyed by having to go and have dinner with his aunts and uncles every couple of months. They hadn't ever even bothered to ask what his favourite pudding was!

Claudia consoled him by telling him that all distant aunts and uncles are the same, and the conversations are all carbon copies: 'How's your love life? How's school going?' All so boring!

But, of course, Toletis couldn't tell his Mum or Dad about all this because they'd get extremely upset.

Claudia and Toletis ate with their legs dangling over the edge of the old trenches that were dug during the war. While they snacked on their peaches, Toletis spoke about the only time he'd ever gotten angry with his Mum.

'I went to school without giving her a kiss when she asked for one, and I couldn't concentrate all day, until I got back home. I kept thinking the worst. So many times I was about to get up from my desk to run home to give her a kiss and then run back to school. Refusing to give your mum a kiss, Claudia, is the worst thing you can do. Don't ever do it, because you end up feeling really rotten and depressed. You're better off letting out some horrific insult.'

He paused, and the silence radiated out, as if all the insects in the valley were holding their breath for a second. 'When I eventually got home, I covered her in kisses. I'd completely forgotten why I was cross because my guilty conscience had been torturing me,' Toletis continued in a very serious tone of voice, the kind that adults use. And then he changed topics: 'Look, the mist is coming. Let's go, Claudia. We need to hurry or we won't get home before it gets dark. Come on, Aeoi, let's go!'

Toletis pulled down the hazel branches, while Claudia was in charge of 'nutting'. As they would say: 'If you can milk a cow, then you can nut a tree.' She would pick the hazelnuts and chuck them into his backpack.

Before nutting a tree, they would crack a couple of hazelnuts between two stones to check if they were ripe. Being careful not to prick themselves on the brambles, gorse bushes and thistles, they scampered across the hillside from tree to tree, collecting their kernels.

Toletis brought up his Mum again.

'You know, I love her so much that sometimes I pretend she's not around anymore, that she's left and that I'm not going to see her again for a really long time, I mean a really long time. I do it so that later on, when I am with her, I appreciate her even more and get even happier.'

The backpack was filling up with round, golden hazelnuts, and the afternoon was filling up with a gentle northerly wind. Holly trees were mingled amongst the hazel trees with the occasional oak sapling poking through. Running along the trenches, there was hawthorn and heather, down below the town with its barking dogs and its slight whiff of cows.

'I think we've got enough. Shall we call it a day, Claudia?'

'Okay … It's a shame we can't wait until it's dark to see the glow worms on the footpath,' she replied.

They still had time to sit quietly for a while, listening to the wind and the distant jangling of grazing cows; watching the grey and violet evening clouds hurry past, and the solitary town below, which seemed so fragile, as if at any moment a storm, tornado or hurricane could effortlessly do away with it, whisking the whole thing off to oblivion without leaving a trace.

Toletis couldn't avoid it. As soon as autumn came, he'd always become more taciturn and melancholy. Once the vibrant glow of summer and Matthias the painter had both left the valley to travel to distant lands, Toletis would become more introverted. Each new day would bring more gloom, and his thoughts and ideas would get all jumbled up. He would stop making plans and would think up stories about loneliness, isolated towns, and boring, uneventful afternoons.

Claudia used to say that even his eyes became smaller.

At the beginning of the autumn, Toletis would walk around as if under a raincloud, and his family often missed a certain cheeky little boy at home. There was even one week when he ran out of words. For a boy who loved experimenting with vocabulary so much, he couldn't stop the silence filtering into him through every little crack, and his only source of joy was watching the yellowy leaves falling from the noisy poplars. He would dodge all the people in the town and imagine a world with no inhabitants, where nothing happened except for the wind and mist rolling in each afternoon.

He hated school on those days because he wasn't allowed to be left to himself, alone, lost in his own thoughts. And because the homework took up valuable hours that could be better spent watching time pass and observing everything sinking into the silence of the night, the winter, the cold. He hated school because it wouldn't permit him to feel his solitude in all its glory, and even, with the screeching call of the tawny owls, to feel a bit scared.

With the melancholy that had just set in that afternoon while on the hillside, it was no surprise that Toletis, after waving goodbye to Claudia, stopped for a while on his own, under the black sky, to look at that night's first few stars. In that stillness, with his rucksack of hazelnuts on his back and his stick in his left hand, his head tilted back, looking up at the sky and the circular moon, he thought again about his Mum:

'I'll get home in a second, and it'll smell of baking, of cakes, and of her. It'll be warm. She'll have her blue flower-print apron on, and she'll smile at me when I appear at the door with the hazelnuts … '

Amenophis also stood watching the moon, which seemed to him to be a delicious bread roll. Dogs also have their thoughts and memories, and Amenophis had a fundamental one saved somewhere between his ears and snout. He was alive and here, thanks to the boy that was now at his side: Toletis.

He remembered his own story perfectly well. His Mum, Sara, had

had a litter of six puppies. As often happens in small towns, the farmer didn't want any more dogs, and he didn't know anybody to give them to. The farmer, a terse and surly man, decided to toss the six little pups into the river to drown when they were only three days old. But Amenophis, the strongest of the bunch, managed to fight the current by grabbing some reeds on the riverbank. A few minutes later, Toletis strolled past. The dog swore he'd never forget the warmth of his hands when he rescued him from the water or the first thing Toletis said to him, 'You're going to be my friend.' And that's how the two of them started their new life side by side.

Amenophis even forgave Toletis for believing that dogs only understood the vowels in words and thinking that the consonants made no difference …

But when he started to daydream, Toletis would sink deeper into a daze than Amenophis, who had a more practical sense of time. So the dog decided to send a loving bark his friend's way to say:

'Come on, you bumboat, let's go home. I'm hungry.' Something like this: 'Grr woof woof garruffff!'

Toletis looked at him, breathed deeply and repeated out loud, 'Marvellous! It'll be warm. It'll smell of cake, and Mum'll be there.'

8

Autumn

THE RICKETY MANSION

It was autumn again, and Claudia was getting ready to visit her Grandmother. The house was several miles away, on the other side of the hill behind a small outcrop in the shape of a castle. Every year Claudia would invite Toletis to go with her because she could see the autumn was bringing down his spirits, and she knew a trip to Granny Ursula's house would cheer him up. The two of them would spend some time with Claudia's grandmother on two dates: her Grandmother's birthday, the 21st October, which was also her saint's day, Saint Ursula, and the 22nd March, the first day of spring. The grownups (Claudia's parents) normally got out of going because they were always so busy finding out how some newly bought technological contraption worked. But Claudia and Toletis were enthralled by Granny Ursula's ancient mansion because it submerged them in sensations that they couldn't discover anywhere else.

For the walk, Claudia always added some theory or other to the conversation. This time, it was her fanciful take on furniture.

'Does the same happen with you Toletis? I find we don't really see the furniture that's always been at home; it's not pretty or ugly. They're just chairs and tables that we walk past without appreciating them. But if one day you actually stop to take in their shapes and colours, they come alive. They have faces with expressions. Well, it happens to me, anyway. Suddenly, for some reason I won't just walk past. You know, I might trip on a sofa and hurt my leg. Then I look at that object and see that it knows much more about me than I know about it. It's watched

me grow, it's followed my footsteps and heard what I've said every day. And I see that it has an expression, perhaps cheerful or tired; that it has cheeks or a fringe; that it's arms are drooping, or that it's legs are akimbo; that it's got a flabby belly or it's puffing its chest out.'

'Gosh, Claudia, you're right. The same thing happened to me a little while back with my Dad's wingback armchair. I jumped as high as I could and landed bottom-first on it. And to show me that it hadn't liked it one bit. It made fun of my ears by flapping its wings at me.'

'You are quite a brute though, Toletis. I bet you hurt one of its springs. But when it's happy that we're noticing it, the furniture seems to give a subtle nod and say, "Hello, Toletis! I'm the table from the dining room," or "Good afternoon, Claudia! I'm the chair that you spend all afternoon sitting on, drawing story boards for when you're a famous actress on the telly." And then it blends back into the surroundings and into its world of half daydreaming-half taking everything in.'

Granny Ursula's ramshackle, rambling mansion was huge and surrounded by even huger oak trees. And, one of those rivers which sound so good when they babble over rocks ran close to it. The four walls were built of stone, with one face spanned by a wooden balcony half-covered with ivy. Smoke always puffed from the chimney.

Within, darkness and silence reigned. Granny Ursula hardly ever opened the shutters, not even enough to let a smidge of light in. It wasn't hard to see that the voluminous, imposing furniture was in charge. There were mirrors, so many mirrors, and enormous complex crystal chandeliers hanging from the high ceilings. The dilapidated mansion was ancient; there wasn't even an extractor fan in the kitchen or a TV in the lounge. Granny Ursula didn't care what a remote control was. She would say that there were already enough things going on, both good and bad, and that she didn't need anything else.

Claudia and Toletis liked it when everything chugged along as normal, year after year; and Granny Ursula liked it, too.

But the best thing, the most intoxicating thing, was the smell of the antique mansion: a mixture of wood, wax and peaches. Second only to recently mown grass, Granny Ursula's decrepit home contained Toletis's favourite smells. He felt them with so much vigour, and they would get so deep down inside him that he wouldn't just smell them; he'd feel them with all five senses. These were things that could be touched, that had taste and that drew his gaze; it was so perfect that if you really paid attention, you could hear the smells. Toletis, enveloped by that essence, couldn't figure out the best way to take it with him. 'We have to learn how to make this smell, Claudia, so we can put it in our houses.'

Granny Ursula's greeting was always the same, 'Oh my goodness gracious me, look how much you've both grown!' Granny Ursula – Claudia never called her Grandma or just Granny, always Granny Ursula – would invite them to have lunch, but practically the whole banquet consisted of desserts, because she knew that's what they liked the most. It was nothing like going to see Toletis's aunts and uncles. 'Your parents can give you soups and stews' is what Granny Ursula would say every year.

Biscuits, sponge cakes, tarts, and muffins of the most varied flavours were spread across the table. The sweetness of the vanilla and the strawberry jams, the soft bitterness of the almonds, and the rich velvetiness of the chocolate.

Granny Ursula took a while to open up, accustomed as she was to darkness and silence. She preferred it when the kids recounted how their year had been, with every detail minutely embellished: both the academic year and their holidays. She paid close attention; you could see it in all the tiny movements of her eyes. They had never met anybody who expressed so much with their eyes. They would open wide, half-close and then close tight; they would shine with happy news and darken with sad stories, like the one about the weak little kitten. They would sparkle, they would get covered in eyelashes, they would get rounder or wider, and her eyebrows would wrinkle down in a frown or ping up with surprise or droop to one side. Sometimes, Claudia and Toletis thought, it even seemed like Granny Ursula's eyes took on the shape of animals or trees, according to the story they were telling her.

The presents came at the end, with the last pudding course: a most intricate, immense trifle through which swam raspberries, redcurrants, wild strawberries, and the odd mint leaf. They would take a present for Granny Ursula from Claudia's parents – a set of table linens and bedclothes, or towels, and a blouse or some shoes – and some craftwork that they'd made in school from clay or card, pieces of wood, pegs, or buttons. Oh! And the jars of bilberries and blackberries from the hillside so that she could make the jams that she'd then spread in her Victoria sponges and Bakewell tarts.

Granny Ursula would then, in turn, lavish gifts on them, but much more original ones: memories. She'd be quiet for almost the entire meal, and then at the end, she'd open up and regale them with stories of her childhood and her adolescence: stories about smugglers and cattle rustlers, witches' parties, and atrocious feuds and grudges between households in neighbouring villages. That day, she told them about the wall clock in the rickety mansion.

'Over there, in that very corner, there used to be a wall clock whose chimes echoed through the whole house. Its pendulum always swung in time; it never lost a single second since I was a girl. The wood was walnut, and the face was decorated with shepherds and their lambs, so well painted that it was as if they were jumping to dodge the ticking hands, playing with the passing of time. There wasn't a clock like it in all the valley … '

'So cool!' whispered Claudia and Toletis, as if they were actually seeing the clock.

'It was the heart that gave the house life; it gave the house a pulse. But one day, an important man from the town who held a high post, but who didn't get along with anybody, reported me because he said I hadn't paid something … some tax or other. And he told two very

serious-looking, burly men who came into the house without so much as doffing their hats. They looked me up and down, and they also looked the house up and down, and they decided to take the thing that meant the most to me: the old wall clock. The billy bigwig left the house telling me, as he looked me dead in the eyes: "Don't you tell a soul, Ursula! This matter is between me and you, and it's sorted." Silence conquered the walls, but I've not fancied getting another clock, even though I know that the tic-toc of a clock is good company, especially during autumn and winter nights. But I've never wanted any other clock.'

That day, Granny Ursula wanted to give them another present, something fantastical that left the kids speechless.

'Come with me. Today, you're both going to get a gift, which I know happens to be the thing you like most about this rickety old house.'

They climbed the stairs up to the third floor with great anticipation: the attic, a strange coop full of cobwebs and wonderful objects. The light was so dim that Toletis felt like the loft was swathed in mist. He loved it! Behind a curtain with blue, green, red, and violet stripes, they saw what it was that gave Granny Ursula's world such an amazing smell.

'Look,' she said to them.

All they could do was stand there with eyebrows raised and mouths, eyes and ears agape in surprise and fascination. Toletis's ears pinged upwards a little. Claudia's hair curled up then straightened out several times as a sign of having been majorly impressed. Behind the blue and green and red and violet curtain, growing between the floorboards was a wellspring of peach trees loaded with yellow-bronze, chubby fruits.

'Go on, pick a couple each.'

Without uttering a word, and moving in reverence and shock, Claudia and Toletis picked the peaches with great care, as though they believed they were going to split, crush or squish them with even the slightest sudden movement.

They stayed in the rickety mansion for another half hour and were incapable of forming a single word. They'd turned into dribbling simpletons who could do nothing other than stare at the magical fruits while shaking their heads and blinking. They were in a dream-world, swaddled in that perfume of wax, wood and peach, as if they were twirling through the rickety mansion on a bed of air, racing through all the rooms like two little clouds melted into the mist of the attic, mingling with the numerous mirrors and golden lamps in the house.

Though they were hardly listening, they did manage to hear Granny Ursula say, in between her chuckling at the enraptured look on the children's faces, that those fruits only gave off their fragrance when it was dark and quiet. And since Claudia and Toletis's parents always had the shutters wide open so that lots of light would come in, the children had no choice but to stash their chubby-cheeked peaches in a couple of shoeboxes.

It was for the best. This way the two of them wouldn't have to come up with any explanations. And every night, sitting on their bed before lights out, each of them would take the lid off their shoebox to have a few moments of breathing in the glorious aroma of the peaches from the tranquil world of Granny Ursula.

9

Autumn

THE WIDE ROAD

'Hurry, Toletis, run! Three new maple trees are sprouting,' an excited Tutan came running over to tell him.

As if he'd just been given a great present, a happy Toletis went to check out what his friend had told him. There, growing just next to the asphalt, were indeed three baby maples.

'We'll have to look after them, Tutan. We're going to have to water them and keep an eye on them until they're strong enough to look after themselves.'

Toletis's nemesis had always been the road that crossed the town. It brought strange people into the heart of his world, screeching past without respecting or appreciating the people, animals, plants, houses, rocks, and landscapes of the valley. Those people just zoomed through everywhere and everything without even glancing at their surroundings.

And it was a very dangerous place. Ever since he was young, his mother had etched phrases into his brain such as, 'Do not play on the road,' and, 'Be careful near that road!'

Amenophis had been learning what the sound of engines and wheels meant, but it had taken more than one fright for it to sink in. When he was a pup, he had to be told off all the time, because he liked to lie down, legs outstretched, on the flat tarmac.

Then the workmen arrived, and the road was widened, which had a frankly awful effect on Toletis. He could hardly bear that the only poplar grove in the middle of the town had been chopped down just to straighten a bend in the road. Toletis never forgave the civil engineers who went up and down giving orders, or the cranes, diggers and steamrollers that obeyed them.

Once the work had finished, Toletis would take a weekly stock of new plants that were sprouting on the verge, hoping that one day in the near future, nature would impose its law, rhythm and aesthetic on the hard grey asphalt.

He had a detailed list noting all the saplings of black poplar, maple and ash that stood beyond the gravel, and also of the brambles, hawthorn and elder bushes. His Grandfather Ra had helped him give the right name to each new find.

So far he'd drawn up a collection of 77 baby plants. But Tutan's news was especially important because up until now they had only recorded four other maples. Four and three made seven: Toletis's lucky number.

The news about the maples had cheered him up enormously.

But the day took a dark and bitter turn when Patricia the kitten, whom Toletis had given so much loving care, got hit by a car and died. She was completely flattened; her poor little body a twisted, jumbled, bloody mess.

The car didn't even stop. The driver probably didn't even notice what he'd done. There was nothing anybody could do to save her. What was a cat with just a few months under its collar supposed to do against the stupidity of a really wide, really straight, really fast road?

Toletis, out of his mind with rage, started to kick the asphalt. He

grabbed a spade from his garden shed and ran back to hit the road as hard as he could, trying to make a hole in the tarmacadam. But it was too dense and thick, like so many people.

Toletis and Tutankhamun armed themselves with courage, they tried to forget the pain and horror for a moment, and, before burying her, they reassembled the splattered body so that it resembled, as closely as possible, a little cat. They placed the head and the neck in the right place, her belly lower down and her back higher up, and then the tail at the end and her little paws at the bottom. They washed her with a sponge and decided to let her lie in the ground next to one of the three new maples. They never said they'd buried Patricia; they always remembered having 'planted' her. And sometimes they wondered whether the maple would grow with flakes on the leaves, like the flakes Patricia had on her skin. Claudia explained to them that it wouldn't, and that, like that day that Ra passed on, they shouldn't be so sad.

Toletis was not one for revenge, but he did have a very well developed sense of justice.

'You lot are a bunch of dumbbells and oafs!' was all he could think to say to the construction workers who had come along to fix some potholes in the road.

'Get out of here, you brat,' they contested with some restraint.

'Bunch of idiots! You've never even imagined that kittens exist. Didn't you know that there are cats that can go into the road? Why does it even have to be so wide?'

'Get lost!' they said impatiently.

'Don't feel like it, don't feel like it, and I don't feel like it! DID YOU WARN PATRICIA? DID YOU TELL HER TO GET OUT OF THE WAY? Well, I'M NOT GOING ANYWHERE EITHER!' shouted Toletis, his wits in tatters and his neck veins popping out with rage.

In the end he did leave, but he headed off to find his friend to concoct an action plan: one of Toletis's brilliant plots.

'We have to do something, Tutan,' he told his friend. 'Let's paint the whole road with big colourful letters in memory of Patricia. Do you think that's a good idea?

'Or we could throw boulders and dry tree trunks into the road so that no cars can get past … Or we could paint all the road signs black … I don't know … We have to do something, Tutan, we can't just let this go … Or every afternoon you and I could stand in the middle of the road where it comes into the city and tell the drivers that they need to do a U-turn, because this road doesn't exist anymore. What about that, Tutan?' Toletis continued plotting.

Tutan, with his permanently sleepy face and his economical use of words, was thinking, and he started blinking slower and slower.

'We have to do something now. There's no time to lose!'

'What for?'

'So that the road doesn't take over the whole valley! Haven't you been listening to me?'

'Sort of.'

'Flibbin' heck Tutan, this is important!'

'That's it!'

'What's it?'

'I know what to do.'

'What?'

'I've learnt how to speak with thrushes.'

'So? We don't have time for bird matters now, Tutan.'

'But, Toletis, we'll ask them for help.'

'How?'

'There are some massive flocks this year. I could ask each one to bring a bit of soil and some seeds. I know they like music by Bach. I'll put it on really loud, and that'll get them going.'

'And then they'll cover the road … '

'Exactly.'

'And then it'll look like a meadow.'

'Precisely.'

'And the cars won't get past. And everything will be green, not grey. You're a legend, Tutan!'

Thousands of thrushes came and went, returned then flew off again, over an entire evening until they completely covered the road with soil and seed.

The next morning, when Toletis, Tutan and Claudia looked out of their bedroom windows they could hardly believe their eyes: the road was buried. Not a trace was left.

Suddenly, it started to rain. But the drops weren't falling from the clouds; it was the huge flock of thrushes that was scattering water. Each bird was bringing a few drops in its beak until they created the downpour.

But it only rained on the strip where the road used to be.

Even though it was autumn, in two days the most varied plants and flowers started to grow. Marigolds and daffodils, violets and clovers, carnations and lilacs, bindweed and honeysuckle all sprouted. What was once grey, rigid asphalt had turned into a soft, fresh, green rug, speckled with vibrantly coloured flowers.

'What a difference compared to before!' exclaimed Toletis.

Even the maple trees seemed bigger, particularly Patricia the kitten's tree, which had started to have a bit of dandruff on the leaves. The mist fell in love with such a unique carpet, and whenever she came to visit the town, she would lovingly tickle it before heading off to the tower of Ra's apple trees.

The civil engineers and construction workers pulled up the green carpet seven times to lay new asphalt. But nobody could compete with the gigantic mutation of thrushes. As soon as the road was restored, the diligent birds high-hoed back to their swirling task and once again spread soil, seeds and droplets of water. The scarecrows were absolutely, laughably useless.

And with practice, the birds' technique got better and better; each new verdant rug, sowed to the tune of Bach, was thicker and more floral than the last.

The town planners had no other solution but to build a new road that went round Toletis's town. They said they'd never seen anything like it, and you could tell they weren't happy about it.

'Tough luck, tough luck, what rotten tough luck,' burbled Toletis, happily.

His town was the only one in the valley with an evergreen carpet between the houses. From then on, all the residents got used to walking around town, from one house to another, barefoot because the leafy carpet, somewhat strangely, was always at the same temperature and moistness. The grass was always even and was meant for bare feet. You can guess who enjoyed it the most: Celemin the shepherd and his goats, of course.

Toletis even wrote a sign that said: 'THIS IS PROPER TOWN PLANNING, NOT THAT OTHER THING. LET'S SEE IF THE ENGINEERS CAN LEARN FROM THE BIRDS.'

10

Winter

SUNDAY MORNINGS

On those short Sunday mornings in January and February, when the hustle, bustle and excitement of Christmas had passed, Toletis was usually to be found in the kitchen, helping to prepare Sunday lunch. The awful weather in his town kept him locked up at home and forced him to swap his plans for flans.

He didn't know how to make stews, and he wasn't particularly into gastronomy, but all week he'd dream of those wintery Sunday mornings he'd spend in the kitchen with his Mum. From the kitchen window, he could see the vegetable patch blanketed with the dull, muted sadness of winter. The plum trees had shrunk in the cold. There was the grey sky and the occasional sparrow. It was only a few degrees above zero thanks to a sun that wasn't the sun, but a heatless blob.

Very early on, his Mum would get the eggs and potatoes on the boil for the Olivier salad. The fresher the eggs, the more effort it took to peel them. The tiled walls would start to bead with sweat, and the kitchen would fill with the scent of parsley and garlic.

Hunks of chicken would slowly brown in the casserole dish. Then the squid would get dressed in its coat of flour; and the tins of albacore, white asparagus, anchovies, and mussels would need opening: a job that Toletis was in charge of, as well as the fruit salad. He loved turning apples, bananas and pears into little chunks as his fingers got stickier.

Toletis wasn't bothered about learning the important cooking skills, like how to roast a chicken or how to prepare lobster bisque. He preferred to focus on the little side jobs, like chucking the olives into the salad or

making fresh mayonnaise, because, in all honesty, what he really wanted was to spend the whole morning mixing up food with his Mum, feeling the spicy warmth in the preparations for the feast.

Of all the Sunday dishes, Toletis's favourite was, without a doubt, the croquettes: massive, filled with béchamel and speckled with pieces of cured ham, soft and cloudy on the inside, crunchy and toasted on the outside. Croquettes which, when bitten into, would leak a deliciously warm ooze that coated your teeth and palate.

He enjoyed getting involved with everything and constantly asking his Mum questions while the windowpanes steamed up with droplets of vapour and the sky filled with ever-denser grey clouds.

The spoon and knife on the right, the fork on the left. The glass out in front and to the right. Bread on the left. Set the plate first with a dish sitting on top of it. The napkin folded into a triangle. Toletis knew the routine well enough.

On normal Sundays, the checked tablecloth; on special occasions, the one with flowers and a lace border which, though uglier, seemed more important.

The bottle of red wine and a jug of water. A few more pieces of bread in the wicker basket for whoever might need a top-up. And salt, in case anybody found something a bit bland, which Toletis's Dad often did.

Aunty Josefina and her husband would always come for lunch on Sundays. Those extra places at the table added to the typical midweek layout and also contributed to that special Sunday meal feeling. Toletis, who the rest of the week would lay the table somewhat apathetically and with no real care, would give it his all on the day of rest. It was part of his ritual, his peculiar ritual.

There was never a day that the memory of his Grandfather Ra escaped him. He would look over at the bulrush armchair, and his eyes would well up with tears. Then, he'd have to go out to the vegetable patch for a moment or two to remember Ra at his best: the Ra of the dizzyingly strong apple tree tower.

On Sundays, Toletis also had the habit of taking an inventory of the kitchen, reviewing all the stock and supplies as if he were the general of an army. He would cast his gaze over the formica table and chairs, the television set and the refrigerator, the begonias and busy Lizzies looking out from their window box, the kitchen sink with its dirty pots and pans, the sweating tiles, the fluorescent light, the Aga where everything was slow-roasted, the shelves where salt, pepper, flour, breadcrumbs, and bay leaves stood at ease, and … his favourite piece of furniture, the Welsh dresser: the one single piece of furniture which stored the odd important letter alongside commemorative cards from christenings and first communions, chinaware, lentils, and his mother's creams for hydrating and moisturising her hands in winter. Oh! And that strange and magical device known as 'the robot', bought by his Mum at a Tupperware-style-ladies-home-selling party in a nearby town. The robot could make sponge cakes, pesto, or seafood chowder with prawns and clams.

Toletis always found something that wasn't where he thought it should be: a colander, a saucepan, a griddle, the whisk. He would then immediately proceed to marshal the rebellious troops. Finally, there was one more thing that, according to him, was not where it should be. It was an intriguing black surface that produced heat without even the slightest glimpse of anything resembling a flame, and it was called the ceramic induction hob. 'What a name!' Toletis would exclaim, 'and people criticise the Wobbegong language … ' Just as well his Mum hardly ever used it. 'Cer-am-ic in-duc-tion hob … Pff!' Toletis repeated. 'It sounds like something from a chemistry lesson.'

The feast commenced. Toletis loved that on Sundays the grown-ups – his Mum and Dad, and Aunty Josefina and Uncle Ramón – would talk about more important matters than during the rest of the week. If the conversation lingered on the typical mumbo jumbo of how fat some neighbour or other was becoming, or how much money Mr What's-his-name must be earning at his new job, Toletis would get nervous. He'd disconnect his ears from the sounds that reached them, and his knees would start to judder up and down, and his thoughts would inevitably escape him; he'd long for the leaves on the trees and the summer sun, and he'd daydream about what Claudia was doing at that precise moment with her parents who were always in a mood, and Tutankhamun surrounded by so many siblings and pulling his 'what's-going-on?' face so they didn't give him any stick.

But if the adults were speaking about how the meadows would feel after the rain and sleet, or if they spoke about a diseased cow, or about a marten or fox that had got into the chicken coop, Toletis would open up his ears. He wouldn't even blink. He would push all his concentration and perception to his ears, and then he would carefully order all the words into the little drawers in his brain, so that he could pull them out later in the afternoon and analyse the conversation in more detail, going back again and again to the dialogues.

He especially enjoyed watching the bouncing heave and sway of Aunty Josefina's voluminous body whenever she laughed. And, she never stopped talking, to the delight of everyone. With her, the squid rings became squibbly-rings, Olivier salad was Bolivia salad, the albacore in brine tasted better than ever, and the rib of beef on the bone looked more blooming lubbly than a magnum of bubbly. Her husband, meanwhile, enjoyed the delights with a plate of roast chicken and a glass of red wine. Toletis loved seeing his Dad nearby and his Mum marching the parade of dishes across the table, dishes which she and Toletis had prepared together and which hardly ever changed from Sunday to Sunday.

In those moments of simple family joy, he even forgot about the melancholy brought by the grey skies and the bare oak trees of January.

Coffee was always accompanied by a surprise that even Toletis didn't know anything about: tea biscuits, or French toast, or little donuts that had been kneaded by the nuns in the walled convent of a nearby town,

or cookies that his mother had made one morning while Toletis was at school, or the shortbread or marzipan that would appear in the shops in the run up to Christmas.

Aunty Josefina seemed to puff up even more with the sweets, and no matter what it was, she would always dunk the treat in her cappuccino. The thing that Toletis liked most about his Aunty Josefina was how much she enjoyed the myriad small details: any little thingamabobble, as she would say.

With that much wine, food and conversation flowing, the little confessions and private secrets would surface, the ones that made Toletis feel a little embarrassed. His Mum was always the most discreet, but Aunty Josefina didn't hold back at all when she was giving chapter and verse on the enormous zit that had germinated on her bottom and which was making her life a misery that week. And Uncle Ramón wouldn't even think twice about pointing out the exact place on the buttock where his wife's inconvenient friend had made its home. All this stuff, though in reality very serious, made Toletis's Dad release the most carefree guffaws. Just seeing him laugh, Toletis forgot how embarrassed he was and became more interested in the revelations.

But, when the troop of dishes that were to march across the tablecloth had done their duty, Toletis automatically suffered a comedown, as if he were on a rollercoaster hurtling downwards. He'd feel dizzy, and he wouldn't feel like laughing or even talking. He just wanted to think and, what's more, think slowly.

As the adults went their separate ways, Toletis would sit on his grandfather's bulrush armchair next to the window and let the faint late-afternoon sun illuminate his face. It was one of the sensations that relaxed him the most: the sun covering his face, entering that winter afternoon languor, and imagining a super Wobbegong world.

When his Mum starting clanging plates and pans together, Toletis would come out of his squid, croquette and fish soup-induced torpor, his muscles would click into gear, and he'd hurry to help his Mum so that – as if he were once again a general that had just suffered an enemy attack – all the tiny soldiers in the kitchen could be dispatched to their rightful places as quickly as possible: clean, organised, mirror-shined, ready to embark on a new battle next Sunday.

11

Winter

THE SNOW IS COMING

It was pretty simple to find out when the snow was going to come. It tended to be around the end of February, and all you had to do was look at the weathervane on the church spire to spot what was going to happen. The cast iron rooster that signalled the direction of the wind would shiver recognisably to announce the coming blizzards. It was easy to see when the cockerel was cold, since his crest would scrunch up and his tail of metal feathers would tremble.

It was time. Toletis would face the north wind head on, his nostrils slightly more flared than normal, his hands in the pockets of his red anorak, and with grand solemnity, he would say, 'Very well, I see the time has come … '

The ritual was repeated each year with few changes. For two days, Toletis would stop doing his homework and become absorbed in drawing what looked like little maps full of arrows and routes, and he would make constant trips up to the attic.

Any clothes that were getting too small for the growing lad would end up in the trunks and chests up in the loft. Toletis had too much of a soft spot for his shirts, trousers, shoes, T-shirts, and pants to simply chuck them out.

Even those items of clothing that were out of fashion – like polo-neck jumpers – deserved a certain respect. They would live in the bottoms of the drawers, forgotten but not discarded. From time to time, these clothes would come out of hiding for one or other of Toletis's plans: making bandages for a wounded cat or for Amenophis, or dressing up for a game with Claudia and Tutan, or building scarecrows so that the sparrows would let the lettuces and tomatoes in the vegetable patch actually grow.

But, above all, they had one specific and worthy role each winter: to keep the town warm in the snow.

Claudia and Tutankhamun, enraptured by Toletis's tradition, were also looting their trunks of clothes. And not just their own, they were taking the stuff being put aside by their parents, too. Whatever they did was never enough for that week in winter – and it was just one week every year – when it would snow in Toletis's town, when the snowflakes would exact a pacifying, silent rest on the natural world, like an interval in the life of the people, animals, plants, and landscapes of the valley.

There were two afternoons of preparation, full of important meetings with Claudia and Tutankhamun to delegate the complex duties.

What they debated most was the matter of the panties and Y-fronts: whether it would be a step too far to put that pair of pink and white frilly knickers, which used to belong to Claudia's Mum, on the fountain in the town square, and Toletis's Dad's old white boxers with red hearts on the gnarled plum tree down at Ra's orchard. In the end, they went with Toletis's idea, seeing as he had the biggest stock of warm clothes.

'Tomorrow, at three o'clock in the afternoon, we need to bring all the clothes to this spot,' said Toletis, finally, in a tone of voice that seemed not to admit that there had been some disagreements.

There they were, at three on the dot, with seven bags of old clothes. Claudia had her hair frizzed in a mane of ringlets to keep the back of her neck out of the cold. Tutan was there with his blue duffle coat, his permanently tired-looking face, and a new pair of gloves covering his big hands. And Toletis had his yellow woollen scarf that half-covered his ears. They'd also given Amenophis a scarf and a sort of canine body-warmer; a long and daunting afternoon was looming.

They started by putting some T-shirts onto the hawthorns that lined the footpath up to Big Hill. They then moved on to three small willows at the side of the road.

'Give these the warmest clothes we've got,' said Toletis. 'Those high-neck woolly jumpers that Santa brought me one year.'

They saved two of Claudia's pretty floral dresses for Aunty Josefina's lilacs.

'This way, as well as being warm and snuggly, they'll feel more cheery,' she said.

And for a group of holly bushes: the checked skirts.

'Wow! Don't they look amazing?!' laughed Claudia.

Tutan and Toletis's trousers ended up on seven little poplars and ashes that were growing next to the river.

'Well, they're pretty skinny in the leg, and they need to plump up in the belly and bottoms for a proper fit,' noted Toletis, 'But, all in all, they don't look too bad.'

An icy wind was blowing, and the three kids' faces grew redder and redder. Aeoi's muzzle was black and shiny, so it didn't turn red, but even so, you could tell he was cold.

They dragged their bags of clothes, which got lighter and lighter, from one side of the town and fields to the other.

Toletis had developed a special sense for detecting which plants were most sensitive to the cold. Even without leaves, he could spot something about them, in the way their stalks shuddered and shrivelled, that told him without a shadow of a doubt, that they needed a scarf, jacket, cape, or some boots more than the other plants.

The plum trees in Ra's orchard were very well looked after with some checked shirts and stripy blouses. The oldest of the lot was dressed up in the heart-patterned boxers.

'The most important thing is that he's warm enough to face the snow storm,' affirmed Toletis.

They gave a pair of pyjamas covered in little bears to the grandson of a very proud oak. And the socks – 17 pairs of them – were shared out among the bare branches that in the summertime were speckled with redcurrants and raspberries.

The youngsters had seen that on the coldest nights the water spouting from the fountain froze into an icicle, so in the end they decided they had to give it the pink panties and a scarf with tassels.

Tutan, Claudia and Toletis used carefully placed pegs and safety pins to hold the clothes on so they weren't blown away by the wind.

'Look, snowflakes are already falling,' warned Toletis. 'We need to

hurry. We still haven't done the black and white storks.'

It was certainly the most complex mission; they had to climb all the way up the dead elm to adorn the storks with their corduroy waistcoats.

'I don't know why they always pick the coldest, windiest place to live. They could stay in Africa a bit longer, and come when it's sunnier here and the afternoons are a bit longer, couldn't they? I really don't understand their traditions,' moaned Claudia. 'And, also, I don't understand why they don't just keep the waistcoats from last year, instead of making us go through all this, every winter.'

'And where are they going to take the waistcoats, Claudia?' asked Toletis, 'you were just going on about how warm it is in Africa. Can't you see they need to go light on clothes and feathers?'

The white stork had the habit of always facing into the wind, and this made it even harder to get him dressed.

The pair of storks were very grateful, they really were. They always saw the children off with a 'thank you' that Tutan had learnt to translate. The three, very politely, replied with a 'you're welcome, see you next year,' which in stork language is something like, 'croto-to-taw, crotaw-toroto crototaw.'

'Bye, Mrs Black Stork, I hope you catch lots of crickets and grasshoppers this year, and take care not to get a cough, because living here, so high up ... ' added Claudia in human language, convinced that the storks could understand at least some of our words from living so close to houses and churches, and listening to so many sermons and conversations.

Once the blizzard had passed, it was time to take stock and collect the clothes that had been shared amongst the surroundings to put them away for next year, so that the sprouting shoots could properly bask in the springtime sun and grow healthily. The kids didn't go up to the black and white storks' nest, because the birds had learnt how to take off the corduroy waistcoats on their own and toss them out of the nest.

From the fountain to the apple trees, from the hawthorns to the oak, from the orchard along the footpath up to Big Hill, the three friends hiked a hearty trail gathering up all their possessions. That year they found the occasional broken hawthorn branch.

'They couldn't cope with so much snow weighing down on them,' explained Toletis. They also spotted an oak sapling that had been mangled and crushed by the wind and snowfall.

'Poor little thing. And to think I'd already given him a name … ' said Claudia.

'What did you call him?' asked Toletis.

'Marky. Poor little Marky.'

The valley had slept for a week. Toletis always compared the falling snow to a lullaby: 'rock-a-bye snowflake,' he would say as he looked out from the window of his house at the silent white landscape.

He still remembered that initial feeling he had had when he was three years old upon opening the shutters one February morning to find it had snowed. He felt like everything had broken, like everything had disappeared, like somebody had rubbed out the trees and mountains and footpaths as if they had all just been drawn in with pencil.

That sensation of an erased landscape had haunted him ever since. Sometimes, he would think, 'Perhaps one year the snow will decide to take the scenery away, melt it all away as the snow melts. And everything would be gone. The white sheet could be peeled back one year, and we'd discover that nothing had been left behind except a huge expanse of rocks.'

Toletis never quite trusted the snow; he worried that over the years, very sneakily, little by little, one flake at a time, it would permanently hide the valley.

That's why, when he saw that everything was more or less as it should be, apart from the odd broken branch or squashed seedling, he felt as though a weight had been lifted from him, and he was always relieved when the landscape went back to having all its usual shapes and colours, ready to embrace the spring.

12

Winter

OLD PHOTOS

On snivelling rainy days, Toletis would often fetch the photographs that were kept in the old biscuit tins and spread them out on the big table in the dining room. Even though he would look at the same images each time, he always found some detail or relationship that had escaped him up to then. The last gift he got from Aunty Josefina had been a digital camera that he loved using to capture the shifting colours of the landscape as the sky changed. But he found the old photos in the biscuit tins somehow enchanting, they took him to other times and places; it was as if they teleported him.

Those long afternoons with the photos were not dedicated solely to contemplating the people, poses, expressions, scenery, and artefacts. Oh no, Toletis would look for strange similarities and weird circumstances that he would almost always make up himself. Occasionally, he would ask his Mum for specific information, 'Who's Mr or Mrs So-and-so?' 'Who was that man married to?' Or 'Was she his girlfriend?'

It was much more fun and creative to draw your own conclusions, to figure out who were brother and sister based on the similarity of their faces or the clothes they were wearing. You could even pretend two random people were father and son or make up your own married couples.

Toletis adorned the stories with comments along the lines of, 'What a boring couple these two are. She looks like a right bossy-boots. I bet she makes his life a misery, and that's why he looks so dead behind the eyes!' 'I'm sure it took this couple ages to save the money for that motorbike;

that's why they're posing so proudly next to it, so that everybody can see it properly.' 'This girl didn't want to have her photo taken that day. She didn't like her hair in braids, which her Mum had done for the occasion, and she didn't like such a horrible dress or those leggings, or those shiny patent leather shoes either! She felt uncomfortable and annoyed. You can see it in her face.' 'This very handsome man was surely the boyfriend of that girl in the photo at the party. They have the same look in their eyes, but it's as if their parents wouldn't let them go out with each other. That's why they're not next to each other, and that's why they've been put in separate biscuit tins … to create a diversion. Don't worry, I will reunite you!'

Toletis put the photos of people together that he thought were a couple or were friends, so that they could live together, away from prying eyes, inside the same biscuit tin.

Between one story and the next, Toletis paid attention to the colour of the sky in the background or the grotesque leftovers of food that appeared in the photos of banquets, weddings, baptisms, and birthdays or the ruddy faces crinkled from laughing.

He focused on the things that most people don't notice. But what struck him most was the expression of loneliness on the faces of so many people.

On those afternoons with short cold days and long boring hours, when he didn't go out with Tutan or Claudia and didn't even have any homework to do … on those afternoons, Toletis and his photographic chums, who would stare at him in almost the same way as dogs stare at people, itching to have the curse of that dumb expression lifted, those picture-people would roll back the clock and turn the images back into flesh and blood. On those afternoons, Toletis and the photo-folks had a mutual understanding of solitude.

But there were three photos that really intrigued him. One was a photo of a girl – Aunty Josefina, but much younger – beautiful, very wholesome and smiley, with her curly hair radiating healthily. She was wearing a white pinafore uniform. It was back when she worked as a waitress in a hotel restaurant. When the photo was taken, she was walking down an opulent staircase, with a big smile and one of her hands resting on the gleaming banister. Behind her, a mirror in an excessively ornate frame reflected the image of one of her colleagues. But, there, with her smock and her smile on that elegant staircase of marble and gold, she was so alone. And it was as if the smile belonged to the mirror, not to her face.

The next photo was of his Grandma; she was plump and had her grey hair tied up in a bun, posing rigidly with her steady gaze in front of a small group of runty poplars, a half-crumbling house in the background and a sky filled with little white clouds, like the ones that come out around the middle of September. For the photo to have a certain air of spontaneity, despite the rigid pose, his Grandma was carrying a basket of onions freshly picked from the vegetable patch. And there she was, so stout and chubby, with her slumped shoulders, her onions and her black

sandals, at the end of summer, and she was also so alone.

The third photo was of another woman. Well, it was of lots of people, but the lonely person, standing aside from the rest of the group, was his Mum. The family photograph had been taken at a New Year's get-together, with everybody holding hands with their arms crossed, ready to sing Auld Lang Syne. It must have been a few minutes to midnight. A few people hadn't joined hands, but they had their arms around each other, giving the group a really tightknit feeling, and everybody's face had a silly expression from the champagne. But his Mum was sitting in a corner, not hugging anyone, just drying her hands with a tea-towel as if she'd just come in from a world of dirty crockery and didn't know what people were chatting and joking about. His Dad was smoking a cigar.

Toletis repeated under his breath that he'd never be alone, that he'd work as a journalist, like the ones he saw on the telly when he watched the news. He would make sure that he was always talking to lots of people, surrounded by people, travelling and getting to know new people and things that would keep him company.

It was quite tricky to find any particularly love-filled or romantic scenes in his family photos. Most of them were cold and premeditated, conventional and lacking in any deep feelings.

But in those snapshots of memories, Toletis always honed in on a young couple who, as if absent from the photo, were gazing deeply into each other's eyes while sitting on a rock in the countryside. It was summer, and she was wearing a delicate, flower-print dress with light ruffles, and her curly chestnut hair was caught mid-flow; the young man sat beside her with his slightly froglike face and his little-boy fringe. Though you couldn't make it out in the photo, Toletis had decided that the hairs on her arm were standing on end from brushing against the boy's arms. A little bit of tanned hairy flesh was peeping out from between his sock and his trouser leg. They were happy people in the thick of a joyful moment. They must have been together for years, but they surely did everything possible to spend an extra minute of every day together, making up excuses and stories to remain in each other's arms for just a little while longer before going back home. Toletis didn't want to think about what they might be up to now, about their current relationship, their arguments and happy moments.

Toletis would always get a nervous feeling in his stomach simply by considering the idea that wonderful situations could come to an end at any moment on any day. He preferred to imagine that this couple had stayed that much in love, gazing at each other so intently. It was, without a doubt, one of his favourite photographs.

He whispered that he would never ever be alone, because he would always be in love. And on a piece of paper, he wrote the name 'Claudia' and drew a heart around it.

In the last bundle of photos, in the newest biscuit tin, there were several dozen photos of Toletis. In one of his favourites, he was sitting in a boat with his bare feet dangling into the water. He remembered that day perfectly: it was the first day that he'd ever been to the beach and seen the sea. Gosh! How seasick he'd been just from watching the waves rolling ceaselessly in and out, in and back out again! He had to sit down straight away because he felt like he was going to get swallowed up by the tide – and back then he still didn't know how to swim. He also remembered a woman who was so fat that every time she went into the water for a swim, everybody else on the beach moved back, thinking the sea levels were going to rise; and a skinny man who was so thin, and his trunks so ill-fitting, that every time a slightly aggressive wave crashed into him, it took his swimwear clean off.

There was another picture of himself that he really liked. He was really young – he would have been a little over a year old. You could hardly see his little chubby body peeking out from behind his Dad's powerful arms cradling baby-Toletis with both tremendous care and strength. In that moment of warmth and protection, father and son felt safe and assured.

There was, of course, a large collection of birthday party photos, of him with his pals surrounded by fizzy drinks, sandwiches, cakes, mountains of crisps, and bowls of sweets; everybody pulling funny faces – their funniest funny faces, of course.

There was another weird one where he was standing with his back to the camera. He'd spend a long while looking at this photo because in real life he never got to see himself from behind. He didn't know what his nape looked like, or his back, or his bottom, or the backs of his ears, shoulders, legs, and arms. He enjoyed looking at this picture because it was him, but it didn't seem like him. It was a stranger with whom he identified in some way. It was a Toletis, but it was another Toletis. He was another person. And that was what he always longed for: escaping his earthly self just for a moment to create new characters, to discover new realms, other personalities, events, stories, lives, worries, thoughts, and dreams.

Toletis used to bring his photo sessions to a close by thinking about what his ideal photo would be like. He would grab a few coloured pencils and a notebook, and would start to sketch what, in his mind, was the perfect picture.

His drawing didn't always come out the same, but it always had forest-covered mountains in the background, an end-of-summer blue sky with little white clouds and wind blowing through the whole rectangular world of the photo.

On this occasion, Toletis drew a girl – Claudia – gazing intently at the photographer. Next to her was Toletis's Mum, wearing an orange flower-print dress and holding a very big handbag. Then, next to her was a very buxom Aunty Josefina.

The three women were standing on a kind of scenic lookout with the mountains in the background; expressions of happiness, freedom and tranquillity adorning their faces, which were a joy to behold. All three of them with their hair angelically swirling behind them from the effect of the wind, giving the scene a cheeky, jovial, spontaneous tone which broke from the austere and stiff poses of so many of Toletis's family

snaps.

That afternoon he decided that his life would never be rigid like an organised, contrived photo; he'd always try to make sure a huge gust of wind was blowing – wind that tousled your hair – and that little clouds were overhead, with good vibes and mountains all around, forming a protective valley ... There would definitely always be mountains in the background.